Amy's Rest

S R SILCOX

JUGGERNAUT BOOKS

ISBN: 978-0-6482991-0-3 (paperback)

First published in 2020
By Juggernaut Books, Australia.

www.srsilcox.com

For my wife, always.

Chapter 1

Georgia Ballantyne stood in front of the floor to ceiling window, watching the CityCat ferries weave their way from one side of the Brisbane River to the other.

This view was why she'd bought the apartment, along with the fact that despite the chaos she knew was happening at street level below, there was no sign of it twenty floors up.

'Poured you a double,' Ren said, handing Georgia a glass of scotch and ice. 'Figured you'd need it.'

'Thanks,' Georgia replied. She took a sip of the scotch and relished the warmth as it slid down her throat. She padded across the carpet to one of the lounge chairs facing the window and sat with one foot folded under her knee.

A white folder with *Wheeler Developments* in simple black type sat alone on the timber coffee table. Georgia picked it up and placed it on her lap. This was

1

the last part of Amy's estate she had to deal with, and once it was gone, she'd finally be able to move on.

Ren folded her feet underneath her on the lounge beside Georgia and cradled her wine glass in her hand. 'Rick's put everything you need in there, and he said you just need to sign the top page where he's highlighted. The builder's ready to go when you are, so it'll be up to you when you want to start.'

Georgia flipped open the folder and thumbed through the paperwork, which included her authority for Rick's development company to deal with the renovations, as well as the final plans and mock-ups from the architect and designer. Estimated costings were at the back, but Georgia didn't need to worry about them. Rick was the one paying the bills. Georgia was going to pay him back from the profit once the cottage was sold.

'Did the builder agree to me helping with labour to save on costs?'

'The builder's fine with it,' Ren replied. 'But you know you don't have to? Rick or Celia could oversee it from here.'

'I know,' Georgia said. 'But I just feel like I should be there to see it finished at least, you know? Get some closure.'

Ren reached across and put her hand on Georgia's arm. 'Are you sure you want to sell it? I know what you and Amy had planned for that place. A change of scenery might be good for you.'

'And what would I do in a place like Elizabeth Creek?' Georgia asked. 'I doubt they'll be needing mortgage brokers up there.'

'Start a business,' Ren suggested. 'Open a bed and breakfast. The cottage would be perfect for it.'

Georgia shook her head and smiled sadly. 'The cottage was Amy's idea and now she's gone...' She blew out a breath. 'There's nothing there for me so I'll be glad to see it go.'

'Okay,' Ren said. 'As long as you're sure.' She squeezed Georgia's arm and took a sip of her wine. 'Rick said the main part of the build will take about four weeks, so that's how long you should plan to be out there. I'll come out and help with the staging, and after that, Rick will take over for the marketing and sale.'

Georgia signed the form and handed it to Ren. 'I think I can manage that.' She took a sip of her scotch, feeling a sense of relief that Amy's estate would soon finally be dealt with after two long years.

Ren folded the form and tucked it into her bag. 'Have you thought about signing up for one of those dating services we talked about? That one where they shortlist potential dates for you looked like a good one.'

Georgia rolled her eyes. 'Ren...'

'No, wait. Hear me out,' Ren said. 'You just said yourself that once the cottage is sold, you can move on.'

'With my life in general,' Georgia explained. 'I'm not ready for dating.' She drained her scotch, stood up and walked into the kitchen.

Ren followed her over and leaned on the island bench. 'It's been nearly three years, George.'

'Two-and-a-half,' Georgia corrected her.

'Point is, you have to get out there sooner or later.'

Georgia splashed water over the bench as she rinsed out her glass and huffed. 'Later's just fine with me.'

'Just think about it,' Ren said. 'You deserve to be happy.'

'I was happy,' Georgia replied.

Ren gave Georgia one of her pitying smiles but didn't say anything more. She gulped down the rest of her wine and handed the glass to Georgia. 'I better go. Rick'll be home with the kids soon.'

Georgia stepped around the bench and pulled Ren into a hug. 'Thanks for helping me out. I don't know what I'd do without you and Rick.'

Ren slung her bag over her arm. 'You're welcome.' As she reached the front door, she turned. 'We might be having a party this weekend. I'll let you know.'

'I might be busy,' Georgia replied.

Ren lifted an eyebrow and Georgia waved her off. 'If I'm going to take four weeks off, I'll have to get all my paperwork sorted at work.' She held the door open for Ren and waited until the lift doors closed before she went back into the kitchen and poured herself another scotch.

She glanced around the apartment she'd shared with Amy for the majority of their relationship. It was smaller than they'd initially wanted, but Amy had made it a home with all her little touches of colour and her knick-knacks. Every time they went on holiday she brought back something small to hang on the wall or sit on the TV cabinet or stick on the fridge. Everything here reminded Georgia of Amy, and selling the cottage meant she'd be able to pay off her legal fees and keep the apartment.

Her eyes fell on the pile of papers on the end of the kitchen table. It was mail addressed to Amy that Georgia had been ignoring. The amount of mail addressed to Amy had dropped off after the first year, but this pile had been accumulating since then. They were mostly just charity brochures and catalogues and Georgia had just gotten to the stage where she didn't want to deal with them anymore.

Signing the paperwork for Rick to start renovations on the cottage had lifted a weight off her shoulders, so she decided that if the cottage was finally being dealt with, then she should deal with Amy's mail.

Her glass in one hand, Georgia scooped the pile up with the other and carried it to the coffee table and began sorting through it all.

Chapter 2

Zoe Jennings spotted the bastard as soon as she walked through the old saloon doors that opened to the beer garden. Frank Dickson was sitting with his work colleagues, laughing over a few drinks.

Typical Friday afternoon. No-one in Elizabeth Creek worked after lunch time on Fridays. Except for the publican and his staff of course.

She stalked over to Frank and stood beside his chair, hands on hips, waiting for him to notice her. Nellie Roebuck noticed her first. Her smile of greeting faded quickly when she realised Zoe wasn't smiling back.

Finally, Frank finished whatever joke he was telling and turned to see what his work mates were looking at. His face drained of colour and he swallowed hard. He knew he was in the shit and Zoe was in no mood to let him off lightly.

'You sold it.' It was a statement, not a question. Zoe already knew the answer thanks to hearing Sally Nugent wondering about the new owner of the workshop when she was filling her trolley with ready-made meals at the IGA.

'I'm not sure—'

'We had a deal, Frank. You said you'd wait 'til I got the deposit.'

'Well I—'

'Well you what? Someone offered you more money? Is that it?'

'Now you just wait—'

'What? Like you said you'd wait? Or do you mean the sort of wait that means you won't keep your bloody word?'

The beer garden had gone deathly quiet and Zoe was aware that all eyes were on her. She didn't care, not one bit. That workshop was hers. Everyone knew it. And in Elizabeth Creek, your word was your contract. Everyone knew that too, except Frank Dickson, apparently.

Frank pushed his chair back and stood up, facing off with Zoe. He was a half-head shorter than her, and he rocked onto the balls of his feet to try to lift himself up to her height.

'You've been telling me for two years you'll get the money, Zoe. Two years! Someone comes along with the money to buy the place and I have to sell it. It's my job.'

'You were selling it to me, Frank. You knew what I was planning to do with it.'

'We didn't have a contract,' Frank said. 'No contract, no sale.'

He smirked at her, practically daring her to bite back.

Zoe's hands balled into fists and it took all her strength not to ring his smarmy little neck.

'Zoe!'

She turned at the sound of her name. Jack rolled across the courtyard and positioned his wheelchair between them so Zoe and Frank both had to step back or get their toes run over. 'Everything good?'

'Does it look like it's good?' Zoe hissed through clenched teeth, not taking her eyes off Frank.

'Righto, calm down. Robbo's asked that you keep your voices down out here.'

'It's not like no-one else knows what's going on,' Zoe said, defying Robbo and making sure everyone within earshot could hear her.

'You should take your sister home,' Frank said. 'Before she gets herself into trouble.'

'You should watch your mouth,' Zoe spat back. 'Or you might end up with a fat lip, just like last time.'

Frank shrank back ever so slightly but he didn't move.

'Hey, come on. Time to go,' Jack said, pushing his wheelchair further between them both and turning it so he faced Zoe.

Zoe stood her ground and glared down at her older brother.

His face softened and he raised an eyebrow. Then he pulled a face and rolled his eyes to indicate that he knew Frank was a dickhead. Zoe resisted smiling but got the hint.

She turned and walked away, Jack rolling alongside her.

As she reached the beer garden doors, Frank called, 'You better keep her under control, Jack, or I'll be calling the Sarge.'

Zoe turned and gave him the finger as Jack nudged her in the back of the leg with his chair and herded her through the pub and onto the street.

As soon as they got outside, Jack turned on her. 'Jesus, Zoe. What the hell do you think you're doing?'

'What do you think I was doing? I was telling him off for selling the workshop.'

'I know what you were doing, Zoe. I mean, why the hell would you make a scene in there? And with Frank? You want to get kicked out? Again?'

Zoe didn't answer.

Jack raked his fingers through his hair. 'Look, I know you don't care what people think, but I do.'

'What's that supposed to mean?' Zoe asked, stopping in the middle of the footpath and folding her arms across her chest.

Jack puffed out a breath and shook his head. 'I'm trying to run a business, Zoe, and going off like that in public isn't helping.'

Zoe clenched her jaw. 'He sold the bloody workshop, Jack. I wasn't going off over nothing. And it's nothing to do with the business anyway.'

Jack put his hands up to diffuse the situation. 'I know, I know. But this new job could be something big and I need you to keep a lid on it.'

'Something big,' Zoe said, shaking her head. She swept her arms around. 'Here? The biggest thing we've ever done since Dad died was helping build the footy club house. And they only gave us that job because Dad was a life member.'

'This is different,' Jack said. 'It could take the business to the next level.'

Zoe rolled her eyes. As much as she loved her brother, working in the family business and Jack's big developer dream was something Zoe didn't share. 'It's just a reno.'

'It's more than a reno,' Jack said. 'It's a great opportunity to work with one of the best in the business. It could mean more work.'

'We've got plenty of work,' Zoe said, although she knew that wasn't exactly true. Elizabeth Creek wasn't booming like some of the other hinterland towns around the place. While Elizabeth Creek was technically on the tourist trail, a rerouting of the highway a few years back had meant that people didn't come through unless they were looking for the place. Work-wise, it meant most of Jennings Constructions business came in the form of hanging doors or patching walls. She started walking away.

'We're starting on Monday,' Jack called after her.

Zoe turned. 'Monday? But I thought we didn't start that one for a couple of months?'

'Time frame's been moved,' Jack replied, wheeling closer to Zoe. 'The project manager's arriving tomorrow morning.'

'Tomorrow?' Zoe shook her head. 'That's not going to work. I've got things to do.'

'You'll still be able to get the kids projects ready for the show,' Jack said. 'Just come and look at the final plans. I could use an extra pair of eyes. Make sure I haven't missed anything.'

Zoe let out a breath. 'Will there be beer involved if I go over the plans with you?'

Jack grinned. 'I think I can rustle some up.'

'All right then.' Zoe uncrossed her arms.

As Jack wheeled along beside her, heading for home, he said, 'This really could be it, Zo.'

Zoe didn't say anything. She'd heard that too many times before, and she didn't want to burst his bubble.

Chapter 3

Saturday morning probably wasn't the best time of day to be travelling to Elizabeth Creek, Georgia admitted, after a three hour road trip turned into five, thanks to getting stuck behind a caravan on a road with no passing lanes. When she finally drove into town, she quickly realised that Rick's assessment of it being small was an understatement. Georgia had been too busy with work to scope out the place with Amy before they bought the cottage, and she only now doubted the decision to believe Amy's reassurances that Georgia would fall in love with the place.

Georgia slowed as she passed the sign that declared that the Business Centre was up ahead. As she turned into the main street, it occurred to her that there didn't seem to be a whole lot of business going on at all. Most of the shop fronts looked like they were painted in the middle of last century and it seemed as though there was two of everything – two butchers, two cafes, two newsagents, two pubs. It seemed like each side of the street was a mirror image of the other.

There was no shopping centre to speak of, no giant supermarket chain and no recognisable fast food outlets, and as she drove slowly through the main street, she wondered what Amy had ever seen in the place. She'd been itching to get out of the city and live a more simple life, but for Georgia, the last few years had been anything but simple.

For the last two years, her life had been dedicated to fighting over the estate with Amy's estranged family. The sticking point had been the cottage Amy had bought on a whim as a promise to Georgia of the new life they'd have when Amy recovered. But Amy hadn't recovered. Within the space of six months, Amy had gone from funny and vibrant, always ready for adventure, to a shell of herself, trying desperately to hold on to the belief that the drugs she was taking were making her better and not worse.

When they'd received the news that Amy had just weeks to live, she'd made Georgia promise to move on with her life and to find someone new when she felt ready to.

Of course, Georgia had promised. She had to really. Who was she to not grant her dying partner's final wish? The problem was, Georgia had no idea how she was meant to move on or if she'd ever be ready to.

That was why this project was so important. Over the next four weeks, Georgia would focus on getting the cottage renovated so it would be easier to sell, and the thing that reminded her of the promises she'd made with Amy over those last few months would finally be gone. The cottage represented a future Georgia could no longer have, and the sooner it was gone, the better.

She followed the robotic directions of the app on her phone to the end of the main street and turned right. Shop fronts turned to unkempt cottages on big blocks of weedy lawns, and soon she was driving past industrial sheds. She slowed down and started scanning both sides of the street until she spotted the sign she was looking for.

She pulled into the driveway and parked in an empty car park. Flipping down her visor, she checked her appearance in the mirror, and then opened her door. The heat hit her like a tonne of bricks. It seemed that, unlike in the city, spring had missed Elizabeth Creek and gone straight to early summer. She let out a long sigh. She hoped the next few weeks would go quickly so she could finally move on with her life.

Chapter 4

Zoe pushed the last of the timber onto the back of her Landcruiser ute, pulled the covers over the top and clipped it down. Once she'd secured the load, she wiped the sweat from her forehead with the bottom of her shirt and called to Nick. 'I'm ready to go when you are.'

'Righto,' Nick called back from somewhere in the shed.

Zoe figured he'd be cleaning his tools and getting them ready for Monday. He'd always been good like that, and the fact they were starting a big new job had him more excited than she'd ever seen him. Their last apprentice had left his stuff everywhere and it was a constant battle to make sure he was ready to go every morning. But Nick? He'd take just as much care with a ten-dollar hammer as he would with a thousand-dollar drop saw. He was a good kid, that was for sure. It'd be a shame to lose him if they couldn't keep the business running.

Zoe dropped a coin into the drink machine beside the shed and pulled out a can of lemonade. She may as well have a cold drink while she waited for Nick to finish up. She'd just popped the top and was about to have a drink when a high-end pretend all-wheel-drive pulled up in the car park. 'Nick, come have a look at this.'

Nick loved cars and she figured he'd get a kick out of this one. It was sleek and black and, judging by the lack of dings and scratches, Zoe guessed it hadn't seen a dirt track since it rolled out of the sales yard.

Nick appeared beside her and when he saw the car he whistled. 'Nice car. Who is it?'

'No idea,' Zoe replied and they both watched as a woman with salon-perfect brown wavy hair and over-sized dark sunglasses got out of the car and walked towards them. Zoe took another drink from the can and watched the woman approach.

Everything about her screamed city-chick and Zoe wondered whether she might be lost. Most people like this woman just drove on through Elizabeth Creek, maybe stopping for fuel and a quick bite to eat on their way to somewhere else more exciting.

As the woman walked towards them, she shoved her sunglasses onto the top of her head. 'Hi,' she said. 'I think I'm after your husband, Jack?'

Nick snorted and Zoe dug him in the ribs before he could say anything. 'Go and grab Jack,' she ordered. To the woman, she said, 'I'm Jack's sister.'

Nick scuttled off to find Jack, who was probably going through paperwork in the office out the back.

'Oh, right. Sorry,' the woman replied.

It wasn't the first time someone had confused her for Jack's wife and it wouldn't be the last. Being a woman and a builder just didn't compute in some people's heads. It used to bother her but it didn't any more. It gave her an element of surprise she could use to her advantage if she needed to.

'You want a drink while you wait?' Zoe asked.

'Sure. If that's okay,' the woman replied, wiping her hand across her forehead.

Zoe pointed to the vending machine. 'We've got water and soft drinks. A dollar each.'

The woman's eyes narrowed. 'I'm fine. Thanks.'

Zoe sipped her drink, taking in the woman's clothes, obviously designer, probably expensive, sticking out like dog's balls in a place like Elizabeth Creek. City. You could smell it a mile away.

Jack rolled out from the workshop, past Zoe and right up to the woman, who Zoe was surprised to see, didn't flinch like people normally did when they first met him.

Jack wasn't exactly many peoples' idea of a builder, having been in his chair now for close to ten years. He was the best builder Zoe knew, better than their father, but what he now lacked in physical ability, he more than made up for in business smarts. Zoe reckoned if they didn't live in Elizabeth Creek, he'd probably be raking it in by now.

The woman stuck out her hand. 'Georgia Ballantyne.'

Jack nodded. 'The Carramar job.'

Zoe almost choked on her drink. Georgia Ballantyne looked nothing like any project manager she'd ever seen before.

'That's right,' Georgia replied. 'I just wanted to go over some time frames and the plans with you before I headed out to have a look at the place.'

'Right. Well. You better come in to the office,' Jack said, wheeling himself around. 'It's air-conditioned.'

As he rolled back past, he glanced at Zoe and nodded at Nick, whose tongue was practically hanging out of his mouth as he watched Georgia walk by.

Zoe grabbed Nick by the shoulder and turned him around. 'Come on. No ogling the clients. We've got a class to run.'

'I wasn't ogling,' Nick replied as he walked to the ute. He stood by the driver's side door, looking hopeful.

Zoe tossed him the keys. 'You take out Mrs Thorburn's roses again, it'll be the last time you ever drive. Got it?'

'Got it,' Nick replied, reefing open the door and climbing in.

* * *

The smell was always the first thing the kids noticed when they walked into the old workshop. It was a heady one of linseed oil and wax and the sweet smells of fresh-cut timber.

Zoe was used to it, of course, but it always brought a smile to her face when she pulled open the big barn door and the kids all took in deep breaths, breathing in the smells that took her back to her childhood.

'Right,' she said, leading the group over to the corner that held the safety equipment. 'Aprons, goggles, earmuffs and gloves,' she instructed, and wandered around helping them with their gear.

Some of them had been before, but there were a few new faces in this group. Nick's younger sister, Dallas, was back which was a good sign. She'd been getting into trouble at school and Nick had brought her down to hang around with him while he helped out a few months back.

He was hoping spending time around the workshop might keep her out of trouble, just like it had with him. While it hadn't been overly successful yet, Zoe saw some of herself in the fifteen-year-old and could sympathise with Dallas's hurry to be done with school.

Dallas also had a good eye for timber and although carpentry didn't seem to be her thing, she'd taken to furniture restoration. Zoe was happy to encourage it, and as she helped one of the group tie up his apron, she said to Dallas, 'There's a dining set I got last week from a garage sale if you want to have look at it. See what you think.'

Dallas shrugged as only a teenager can. 'I'll see.'

Zoe didn't push it. It was hard to believe she was related to Nick, who could be like a puppy dog at work sometimes the way he followed her around on the job, waiting for the next thing to learn or do. Dallas did things in her own time, and Zoe had learned quickly that she had to decide for herself if she wanted to do something or she wouldn't do it at all. Stubborn. Zoe could relate to that.

She did a quick head count and checked that each of her class had their safety equipment and then led them over to the timber workbench that filled the centre of the room.

'Right. Boxes,' Zoe said, sliding a small wooden box into the middle of the table. 'Looks easy, right?'

She got a few nods but mostly the kids were non-committal. They were always quiet the first few times they came to Zoe's classes.

'Well, they are pretty easy to make once you know what you're doing. Did everyone bring something to put in their box?'

The kids held up various items from marbles to a book and Zoe nodded thoughtfully. Out of the corner of her eye, she saw Dallas sizing up the table and chairs at the back. She smiled to herself and brought her attention back to her class. 'We need to know how big your boxes are going to be. Nick?'

Nicked stepped forward and placed a container of pencils on the bench and started handing out tape measures.

'Let's get measuring,' Zoe said.

She and Nick wandered around the class, helping them with their measurements and drawing rough sketches of their boxes. Once they were done, Zoe said, 'Who wants to cut some timber?'

Ten hands shot up in unison and Zoe grinned. It was always the tools that got them excited.

'We better go choose some then.' As she led them over to the pile of timber she kept for her classes, her phone rang in her pocket. She asked Nick to help the kids choose their pieces while she answered it.

'Hi, Jack. What's up?'

'Have you got time to take Georgia Ballantyne up to Carramar?'

Zoe pulled a bit of timber off-cut from a pile and handed it to Nick. 'I'm in the middle of a class.'

'It doesn't have to be right now,' Jack said. 'Just some time this arvo.'

Zoe glanced at her watch. Classes normally ran for about an hour or so but she liked to let the kids hang around for as long as they wanted afterwards. 'I can maybe do something around two, three o'clock?'

'That should be okay. I'll give her a call and confirm.'

'Text me where I need to meet her,' Zoe said. 'I have to go. I've got kids wanting to start building their boxes.' She heard Jack chuckle on the other end of the phone. 'What?'

'You're just like the old man,' Jack said.

'One of us has to be,' Zoe teased.

'I'll check in with you later,' Jack said and hung up.

Zoe shoved her phone into the back pocket of her jeans and turned her attention back to her class.

As she and Nick led them back to the workbench, chattering about what sort of boxes they were going to build and whether they'd be entering them into the show this year, she glanced over at Dallas again.

She was leaning low over the table, running her hand along the top to gauge its level. With any luck, that dining setting would keep Dallas busy for at least a couple of weeks, depending on how much time she spent on it.

Zoe guessed that Dallas had no idea she knew about her sneaking into the workshop after school and after hours. As long as she put things back where they belonged, Zoe couldn't care less. Sneaking into Zoe's workshop was far better than the alternative.

Chapter 5

After going over the renovation plans with Jack Jennings and booking into her motel, Georgia decided to see how good the coffee was at the local café while she waited for the builder, Zoe, to take her out to Carramar.

She was embarrassed to have mistaken Zoe for Jack's wife, especially when she discovered she was the head builder for Jennings Construction. She knew how frustrating it was when people assumed she was an assistant even though she was a manager.

At the counter of the café, Georgia ordered a skim-milk latte and settled on a seat in the back corner so she could people watch. The old armchair she chose was surprisingly comfortable considering its worn appearance, and Georgia sank into it, casting her eyes around the space.

It was small and rustic, typical of the sorts of cafes she and Amy had found on their travels up into the hinterland. They'd never made it as far north as Elizabeth Creek so it was comforting, in a way, that this café was one that Amy would have enjoyed.

Magazine-covered coffee tables and old leather couches intermingled with the usual faux-timber-topped café tables and white-washed timber chairs.

There were a handful of customers inside when Georgia arrived. Locals, judging by the way they greeted each other. They seemed friendly enough, but didn't bother her, which was fine by Georgia.

She wondered whether it was usually so quiet and her financier's brain kicked in, questioning whether she'd made the right decision in gambling so much of Ren and Rick's money on the renovations. The property market was supposed to be steady up here, but Rick had assured her it was the city market they were trying to entice. She had to trust his instincts. Property development and renovation was his domain, after all.

Her coffee arrived in a small glass and Georgia stirred in two teaspoons of sugar before closing her eyes and taking a sip. Better than she was expecting, though not nearly strong enough. She'd have to remember to order a double-shot next time.

'You'll have to get that to go,' a voice said nearby.

Georgia looked up to see Zoe Jennings standing by the chair across from her. She was wearing the same jeans and t-shirt from this morning, albeit dirtier, and her dark hair was curled around her ears from under a tatty and stained trucker cap with a stylised 'JC' embroidered on it. 'I'm sorry?'

'If you want to take your coffee with you,' Zoe said. 'You'll have to get it in a to-go cup.'

'Right,' Georgia nodded, standing and picking up her coffee and taking it to the counter. Blunt, Georgia thought. Nothing like her brother, who was warm and engaging. The two of them seemed to be chalk and cheese. Jack seemed put together with his neatly trimmed beard and short-cropped hair. Zoe, on the other hand, looked like she was a month past needing a haircut, and Georgia wouldn't be surprised if she was one of those people who lived in a single pair of jeans.

Georgia handed her glass to the barista who took it, poured it into a take away cup and clipped on a lid. He handed it back to Georgia, and then handed a cup to Zoe.

'Thanks, BJ,' Zoe replied. Without saying anything more, she turned and headed out the door.

Georgia figured she should probably follow her. 'I'd be happy to go in my car,' she offered, hastening her pace to catch up.

'Mine's fine,' Zoe replied.

'Are you sure?' Georgia asked. 'Mine's probably more comfortable.' If the state of Zoe's clothes were anything to go by, Georgia wasn't sure she wanted to get into Zoe's car.

'I'm sure,' Zoe said. 'You'll thank me later.'

When they reached the ute, Georgia resisted the urge to recoil. She recalled the constant mess her father's work ute was in, and it wasn't nice.

When she got in, however, she was pleasantly surprised. It seemed Zoe took good care of her car. It was almost as clean inside as her own car, if you overlooked the pile of cassette tapes sitting on the passenger's seat.

Zoe must have seen Georgia looking at them because she said, 'Sorry, let me just get those,' as she grabbed the cassettes and shoved them into the glove box.

'I haven't seen a cassette in years,' Georgia said as she climbed up into the cab.

Zoe grunted a reply as they drove off.

'I'm sorry I thought you were your brother's wife earlier,' Georgia said.

'Happens more than you think,' Zoe replied, taking a corner a little too fast for Georgia's liking. 'We don't really look much alike, so it's an easy mistake to make I guess.'

They drove through the main street in silence, and turned off onto the highway that ran west.

Out of the blue, Zoe asked, 'Why Carramar?'

'Sorry?'

'It's not something a company like Wheeler Developments would be interested in,' Zoe said. 'I was just curious about why they've bought it.'

'Oh,' Georgia said, stalling for an answer. She wasn't sure she wanted to tell a perfect stranger the truth about the cottage, not yet at least, so she settled for a half-truth. 'It seemed like a good idea at the time, I guess.'

Zoe gave her a sideways glance. 'Have you been up here to see it?'

'No, first time,' Georgia confessed. Amy had bought the cottage after a day trip to the hinterland with her friends, and the one trip they'd had planned to come up and see it together had been derailed by a sharp decline in Amy's health. She glanced at Zoe who kept her eyes on the road, but had an amused look on her face. 'Why?'

Zoe shook her head. 'No reason.'

They turned off the main highway onto a single lane bitumen road lined with tall, brown grass and within a few minutes they were turning off onto a dirt road that seemed to have materialised out of nowhere.

She slowed the car as they drove over a cattle grid and past a sign that proclaimed the property to be 'Carram', the 'a' and 'r' apparently having rusted away.

'See why I didn't want you to bring your car?' Zoe asked as she slowly picked her way over a track rutted by erosion.

Georgia nodded.

'First thing we'll do,' Zoe said. 'Is get the road graded so it'll be easier for the trucks to get in and out. Might have to widen it a bit too, but you'll be able to get your car up by the end of the week. If we'd had more notice, we could've had it done already but we'll deal with it.'

Georgia wondered if Zoe was having a go at her, but decided to ignore it. The last thing she wanted to do was to pick a fight with her builder before they'd even started.

They continued on, driving over a concrete causeway on a dry creek bed. 'This goes under when we get good rain,' Zoe said. 'You might want to think about building out the causeway into a proper bridge so you don't get stuck in or out.'

'I'll consider that. Thanks,' Georgia replied. She couldn't remember what had been budgeted for road works so she made a mental note to check with Rick. Whatever would get her the best return on the sale would be what she decided to do.

The trees thinned out to a wide grass paddock dotted with broken fencing. There were a couple of old caved in sheds not far from the track and a sad-looking windmill missing half its blades in the distance. It looked nothing like the original photos from two years ago.

They ascended a hill and pulled up on a patch of dirt in front of an overgrown bougainvillea bush that hid almost the entire front of the cottage.

'That will have to come out,' Georgia said, jumping down from the ute and shutting the door.

'Not a fan of bougainvillea?' Zoe asked as she crunched across the gravel.

'Not when it's right there,' Georgia replied. She looked back to where they came from, and had to admit that the view was quite spectacular. It would be even more so if the paddocks were lush and green. Driving up the dirt driveway, the cottage felt a million miles from anywhere, but in the distance, she could see the edge of town.

She turned back to the cottage and shielded her eyes from the afternoon sun. Two big sheds cast their shadows from the back of the cottage. They were the ones Rick had suggested she could turn into an events space and a bunk house in the full plans if she wanted to turn it into a bed and breakfast. She'd decided to use the potential of those sheds as a selling point, and just do the cottage renovations. Although the full development might get her more money at sale, she'd opted for the plans that would take the least amount of time to complete.

Georgia followed Zoe to the front of the cottage, pulled out the keys and tried several in the front door before she found the right one. She unlocked the door and pushed. It stayed shut tight.

Zoe stepped in beside Georgia. 'Let me have a go.' She leaned into the door with her shoulder, pushing until it opened. 'It's probably warped and sticky from being closed for so long.' She stepped back to let Georgia through first. 'Mind the floorboards. They might be a bit rickety.'

Georgia stepped tentatively into the gloom. Thanks to the bougainvillea and the rest of the overgrown front garden, the front room was a far cry from the sun room it was meant to be.

There were two windows on each end and a row of filthy louvre windows on the front wall that let in hardly any light.

She stepped through another open doorway and coughed out a breath. 'What on earth is that smell?' She covered her mouth and nose with her hands.

'Probably a dead possum,' Zoe replied. 'Wouldn't be surprised. They sneak in through a hole in the roof and then sometimes the silly buggers can't get back out again. Die right there in the roof. Or,' Zoe continued, scratching her cheek. 'Could be a carpet snake. They love it up there in the ceiling.'

Georgia shuddered at the thought of a snake in the ceiling, even if it was dead. She pulled a face and tried not to breathe too deeply. This was going to be a much bigger project than she first thought.

Chapter 6

Zoe hadn't been to Carramar since the old hermit who'd lived there had died a few years back. She'd gone to the estate auction with Jack to see if there was anything of interest for the workshop, but they'd come home empty-handed.

Everything that was worth something had sold back then except the property itself, and whatever was left was scavenged. Zoe was surprised the old cottage had lasted so long.

It was in such a state of disrepair, she was sure someone would buy the block for the land alone, knock down the cottage and build a new house. The outlook was amazing, especially after good rain when the paddocks greened up. She was glad that whatever plans the developer had for Carramar, it included restoring the old cottage, rather than knocking it down. There was always so much history hidden under the paint and behind walls in old houses. It'd be a shame to lose it.

She followed Georgia as she picked her way slowly through the cottage, taking the occasional photo on her phone. Though most of the furniture and fittings had been taken away years ago, there was still the odd upturned chair or bric-a-brac strewn around the place.

It wasn't a huge cottage, just two bedrooms and a couple of sun rooms, but it was typical of the era it was built. The front veranda had been closed off at some point to create an extra room and the back of the cottage had been bricked in to enclose the kitchen and bathroom, but the rest of the house looked to be original.

They walked through into what would have been the lounge room with a bedroom off to each side. Georgia peered through the doorways of each and then wandered through to the back room, which had been turned into a kitchen and dining area. To the left was the bathroom.

'We can save that tub if you want,' Zoe said, pointing to the old cast iron bathtub in the corner.

'Won't a new one be better?' Georgia asked, screwing up her nose.

'That cast iron one is worth its weight in gold. A bit of resurfacing and it'll be good as new,' Zoe said. The thought of that old tub going into a skip bin horrified her.

'There's no toilet,' Georgia said.

'It's out the back,' Zoe replied. She unlocked the back door, which was easier to open than the front, and pointed to a dilapidated, weathered building that stood on a slight lean about twenty metres away. 'That's it there.'

Georgia stood beside Zoe and peered out the back door. 'What? That shed?'

Zoe nodded.

'But why outside?'

'You've never seen an outdoor dunny before?' Zoe asked.

Georgia shook her head, a horrified look on her face.

'That's how things used to be,' Zoe explained.

'But how…?'

'I don't know about this one, but they were usually a can or something like that. You did your business and scattered sawdust over the top.'

'And then what?'

'And then what, what?' Zoe asked.

Georgia screwed up her nose. 'Wouldn't it get full? The can?'

'Yeah, but out here, they'd have dug a pit somewhere and—'

Georgia put her hand up and shook her head. 'On second thoughts, I don't want to know.'

'It's unlikely it'll be close to the house, if that helps,' Zoe said, trying hard not to laugh at Georgia's obvious disgust.

Georgia pulled a face and turned around, apparently unable to even look at the old toilet. 'That's revolting.'

'Everyone had them.'

'Well that will definitely be going,' Georgia said.

'Sure you don't want to keep it?' Zoe asked, only half joking. 'I mean, something like that definitely adds to the character of a place like this. You don't want to get rid of too much of that sort of stuff if you can help it.'

She was sure Nick would come up with something fun to do with the old outdoor loo.

'Definitely not,' Georgia replied, and walked down the back steps.

Zoe smirked as Georgia took a wide arc around the outdoor toilet and headed for the sheds at the back. 'City chicks,' she muttered to herself as she followed Georgia out the back.

When they'd finished inspecting the sheds, they walked back around to the ute where Zoe pulled out the plans and placed them out on the tail gate.

She orientated them so they matched the orientation of the cottage.

'So we're opening the front veranda back up,' Zoe said. 'And apart from the refurb in the original cottage, we're adding an extension on the back to increase the living space and add a master bedroom and ensuite.'

'So what's first?' Georgia asked.

'Stripping out the walls and ceilings and seeing what's in the roof,' Zoe replied.

'So, you're gutting it,' Georgia said.

'Well, that depends what we find. I'm hoping we get to save most of it. The VJ's look like they're in pretty good nick, but we won't really know until we strip it back.'

'VJ's?' Georgia asked.

'Vertical joints,' Zoe answered, wondering why Georgia, supposedly the project manager, didn't know that.

'Right,' Georgia replied. 'So Monday will be demolition?'

'And road works,' Zoe replied. 'Nick and I will come up early to beat the grader and get started on the demo, and we'll have a couple of labourers in giving us a hand early on. Should take us a day or two to strip the place back and see what we've got.'

'Should I meet you somewhere Monday morning then?' Georgia asked.

'Why?'

'To come up for the demolition.'

'You don't have to be here for that,' Zoe said. She knew Jack had negotiated with the developer for Georgia to do some labouring work, which Zoe wasn't exactly happy about, but it was Jack's call. There'd be plenty for her to do later on in the build, but she'd just be in the way while they were demoing.

'It's fine. I'm happy to help,' Georgia replied.

'Nick and I will be fine,' Zoe said. 'You can stay in town, sleep in. You can come up once the demo's done and the road's fixed. Besides, it's a construction site so there's safety issues to consider. Have you got all your PPE?'

'PPE?' Georgia asked, crinkling her nose up.

For a project manager, Georgia Ballantyne seemed to be absolutely clueless. Zoe wondered whether this was her first job. She'd make a point of talking to Jack about that when she saw him next. If this Wheeler Developments company was fair dinkum, they shouldn't have sent their least experienced employee.

'Personal Protective Equipment,' Zoe explained. 'Hard hat, steel caps, work clothes.' She ticked them off on her fingers.

'I can get a hard hat,' Georgia replied. 'And my clothes are perfectly fine.'

Zoe looked Georgia up and down, her eyebrows raised. She very much doubted that Georgia's idea of work clothes were the same as hers. 'You can't come on site dressed like that.'

'Like what?'

'Like you're stepping onto a photo shoot. You'll get plenty of photos for your social media, don't worry about that.'

Georgia crossed her arms and drew herself up. 'I don't need social media photos.'

'Look,' Zoe said. 'If you're coming on site, you'll need steel caps at the very least. And if you're going to be working here, then you should get yourself some work pants or jeans and shirts.'

'I have jeans,' Georgia said. 'And they're more than suitable.'

'Yeah, well, I'll be the judge of that,' Zoe said. She looked down at the plans. 'So I've got some windows at the workshop—'

'What gives you the right to decide what I can and can't wear?' Georgia asked, glaring at Zoe.

Zoe turned to face Georgia and crossed her arms, mirroring her pose. 'I'm the site foreman and what I say goes.'

'Well,' Georgia said, sticking out her chin. 'I'm the one paying you, so what I say goes.'

Zoe resisted the urge to roll her eyes. Obviously, Georgia was going to be one of those clients. 'My site,' she said, pointing at her chest. 'My rules.' She gathered up the plans and put them back into the folder and closed the tailgate. 'I think we're done.' She opened the car door, got in and turned the key.

She could see Georgia glaring at her in the rear view mirror. She finally stomped around to the passenger side, flung open the door and climbed into the seat, slamming the door. She reefed her seatbelt down, taking a couple of goes before it let go, and clicked it in. Then she sat staring straight ahead and crossed her arms.

As Zoe drove back down the driveway and into town, she thought about all the ways she could make this job go faster so that she didn't have to put up with another painful client like Georgia Ballantyne. Four weeks with her was going to feel like a life time.

Chapter 7

'Did Rick even meet them?' Georgia asked Ren later that night. She'd pulled out all the clothes she'd brought with her and had them lying out on the bed. Surely her jeans and button-up shirts would be suitable for the work site?

'Celia contracted them,' Ren replied. 'They're the best in that area, she said. Why?'

'The builder's a bit, I don't know. Arrogant?'

'Wouldn't be the first one. Most men are, builders or not. Even Rick can come across as arrogant sometimes.'

'He's a she,' Georgia said.

'Really?'

'Zoe,' Georgia confirmed. 'Sister of the owner of the business.'

'Huh, well there you go,' Ren replied. 'What did she say to get up your nose?'

'She told me she wouldn't let me on the work site unless I get the proper clothing,' Georgia replied.

'You don't have steel-caps. I'm not surprised,' Ren said with a laugh.

'I'm supposed to be keeping an eye on things,' Georgia replied. 'Aren't I supposed to be on site?'

'Of course you are, but you need to get yourself some boots. It's an insurance thing,' Ren explained.

'What? In case I kick my toe or something?'

'Exactly.'

'You're supposed to be on my side,' Georgia said.

Ren sighed. 'Just go and get some boots, George. And anyway, you don't have to be there every minute of every day. They're builders. They know what they're doing.'

'If it's that easy, why did I even have to come up here in the first place?'

Ren chuckled on the other end of the phone. 'You wanted to get closure, remember?'

Georgia snorted out a breath. 'Yeah, well, maybe I should have listened to you and let Rick pay for a project manager.'

Ren's voice softened. 'I'm sure everything will be fine. Look, I can see if I can get some time off and come up.'

'Could you?'

'Of course. Rick's folks should be fine to take the kids. Besides, I could use a break myself.'

Georgia dropped down onto the end of the bed. 'Is everything okay?'

'Just the usual,' Ren replied. 'Kids are driving me nuts, Rick's leaving his clothes all over the place, you know how it is.'

'Sounds like you need a break,' Georgia said.

'It's all right for you, not having anyone else to worry about and taking off to the country at a moment's notice,' Ren replied.

The light tone in Ren's voice told Georgia it was meant to be a joke, but it still hurt.

'Sorry,' Ren said quickly. 'You know what I meant.'

Georgia plastered on a fake smile, hoping Ren could hear it in her voice. 'It's okay, I get what you meant.'

'Anyway,' Ren said. 'You haven't told me much about the house. How is it?'

'It's in pretty bad shape,' Georgia admitted. 'You got the photos I sent through?'

'It's not that bad,' Ren said, her voice soothing. 'If you put in some hard work on it, show it some love, someone's bound to fall in love with it.'

Georgia couldn't help but feel like Ren was talking about her, as much as the cottage. She pushed her clothes into a pile and lay back on the bed. 'I'm glad one of us is optimistic. The builder—'

'Zoe,' Ren corrected.

'Zoe,' Georgia said, rolling her eyes even though Ren couldn't see her. 'Said there could be wood rot and water damage. Have we factored that into the budget?'

'You'll have to talk to Rick but I'm sure he would have,' Ren replied. 'He's all over it, don't worry about that.'

'Just out of curiosity, why didn't Rick and Celia suggest I just knock it down and build a new place?'

'Character,' Ren replied. 'You can't replicate it. And like Rick says about his apartments, sex sells.'

Georgia laughed. 'What on earth has sex got to do with it?'

'Everyone loves a little romance, right? What did you think of when you first saw the mock-ups of the cottage renovations?'

'That Amy would've loved it,' Georgia replied. She closed her eyes and pictured the view across the paddocks from the front of the cottage, and tried to imagine what it would have looked like had Amy been standing there with her. Her heart ached at the thought of it.

'Exactly. You can't get that in a new house. The romance of the old cottage is what's going to sell it when you're finished with it.'

'You're probably right,' Georgia admitted. She glanced at her watch. It was after eleven. 'I should go. It's been a big day.'

'Have you got any plans for tomorrow?' Ren asked.

'Apart from finding a pair of work boots?' Georgia asked, hoping Ren could hear the sarcasm in her voice.

'Are shops open on Sunday there?' Ren asked.

'Probably not,' Georgia replied. 'I can't imagine there's too much else to do around here on a Sunday, so I might take a drive, get a feel for what's around. Maybe find some selling points we can use when I put it on the market.'

'Great idea,' Ren said. 'We'll talk on Monday?'

'Will do,' Georgia replied. She hung up and dropped her phone beside her on the bed and looked up at the ceiling.

'Four weeks,' she muttered to herself. 'All going well, everything will be finished in four weeks and I can get it on the market and get on with my life.'

She pushed herself up off the bed, gathered up her clothes and dumped them back into her suitcase and headed for the bathroom. She just had to keep things together until Ren arrived.

Chapter 8

Zoe flipped the steak on the barbecue and took a swig of her beer while Nick and Jack looked on. She never understood why men seemed to gravitate to the barbecue. Maybe it had something to do with raw meat and fire that went back millennia.

Or maybe they just wanted to avoid the kitchen at all costs. Whatever it was, she was the designated barbecuer in the family, since Jack couldn't seem to cook a steak to save himself. Not like their father could at least.

'What's happening with the dunny?' Nick asked.

'It's going,' Zoe replied. She flipped the sausages, one by one, and put all but two of them onto a tray. She left the last two to burn just like her niece, Josie, liked it. She flat-out refused to eat a sausage unless it had been burned to a crisp thanks to her older brother's teasing about eating animals and making sure they were dead first.

'I could do something really cool with it,' Nick said. 'I mean, we could even make it into a proper outdoor toilet.'

'I know,' Jack said. 'But the client wants it gone and that's what matters.'

Zoe checked the steak and the remaining sausages. Satisfied that the steak was cooked just on the medium side and the sausages would pass the char test, she turned the gas off on the barbecue and carried the meat to the table.

'Meat's ready, Mol,' Jack called.

Molly looked up through the kitchen window and smiled. 'Come and give me a hand with the salads, will you Nick?'

Nick put his beer on the table and headed inside.

'We need a side project for him,' Jack said, jabbing his thumb at the empty doorway Nick had disappeared into. 'He's been driving me crazy at the shed.'

'I know,' Zoe replied. 'I'll see what I can dig up. Apart from this Carramar job, everything else is small stuff.'

'What about helping you out more with the kids?'

'He gets too impatient with them,' Zoe replied. 'He's good with them, just that he wants to do things for them instead of letting them do stuff themselves.'

Jack chuckled. 'Reminds me of a certain little sister of mine.'

Zoe rolled her eyes. 'I'm not in my twenties anymore, Jack.'

'Yeah, well, you still haven't grown out of some of your immaturity.'

'Have too,' Zoe said and when Jack raised an eyebrow, she poked out her tongue.

Jack shook his head and laughed and then sucked in a breath. 'I'm worried we're going to lose him.'

'What do you mean?' Zoe asked.

'We're not getting enough work in to keep us going. I'm thinking I might have to start calling in some favours with some other builders to find him work to finish his apprenticeship once this job's over.'

'I thought this job was going to bring more?' Zoe asked.

'I'm hoping it does, but there's no guarantee, so I have to think about a Plan B,' Jack admitted.

'Shit, Jack. I didn't realise we were that bad.'

'We're not, not yet, anyway. That's why the Carramar job's so important.'

Before Zoe could say anything more, Molly and Nick returned from the kitchen and placed trays of vegetable bake and salad on the table. Josie and Ryan ran up from the yard and jostled each other before dropping onto the bench seat either side of Zoe. Zoe put the two burned sausages onto Josie's plate.

'Are they dead enough?' Ryan teased. Zoe dug him in the ribs and he just grinned but got the hint.

'Are you excited about the new job?' Molly asked as she spooned vegetable bake onto Josie and Ryan's plates.

'Better than just hanging doors and the other odd jobs we've been doing,' Zoe replied.

'It'll be great for business,' Jack said, pulling a steak onto his plate and handing the tray to Nick. 'Might lead to more jobs like it. The developer is pretty big in Brisbane.'

'That's great, hon,' Molly said, smiling at Jack.

Zoe watched as Jack smiled back at his wife and then glanced at her. From the look he gave her, Zoe knew Jack hadn't discussed the business problems with Molly.

'Speaking of the developer,' Jack said. 'I got a weird email from them this morning.'

'On a Sunday?' Molly asked.

Jack passed the barbecue sauce to Zoe. 'They said you told Georgia she couldn't be on site until she, and I quote 'sorted out her safety equipment'. Is that true?'

Zoe rolled her eyes. 'It's a safety thing, Jack. You know that. She hasn't got any steel caps and if she's going to be on site, she's got to have them. I just told her she needed to get some, that's all.'

Jack shook his head. 'This is a big deal, this job. You can't talk to our clients like that.'

'Like what? I just told her the safety requirements, that's all.'

'How is she meant to get boots here?' Molly asked.

'She can go to the outfitters like the rest of us,' Zoe said. She swiped her steak through a pile of sauce and shoved it into her mouth.

Molly clicked her tongue and shook her head. 'They have to order your size in whenever you get new ones.'

Zoe stabbed at her steak. 'So?'

'So?' Jack said. He pointed his fork at Zoe. 'It'll take her two weeks to get them in, you know that. She can't be off site for that long.'

'She could drive back to Brisbane and get a pair,' Nick said before piling food into his mouth. He looked around at everyone like he'd just been the most helpful of all of them.

'She could,' Zoe agreed.

'Nonsense,' Molly said. 'I'm sure you've got a spare pair around somewhere.'

Zoe scoffed. 'I'm not giving her a pair of my boots.'

'Why not? That would tide her over 'til she got her own pair at least,' Jack said.

'I don't even know what size she is,' Zoe said. She stabbed a piece of steak, slathered it in vegetable bake and shoved it in her mouth.

'Even if they don't fit,' Jack said. 'If you offer her a pair of yours, at least we can say we tried to get her on site. And if they do fit, well, then that's even better.'

Zoe glared at Jack but didn't have anything else she could say. She did have spare work boots at home, that wasn't the point. Georgia Ballantyne was obviously inexperienced and Zoe doubted she'd last past the demolition stage before she got bored and went back to the city. Those renovation shows on television had a lot to answer for.

'Fine,' she said, finally. 'I'll see if I can find a spare pair and offer them to her.'

'Good,' Jack said.

'Can't guarantee she'll take them though,' Zoe said. She took a swig of her beer. 'And anyway, why are we talking about work when we should be talking about Nick's foray into modelling?'

'That's right. Have you got a partner yet for the Mister Elizabeth Creek competition?' Molly asked.

'Tara's going to do it,' Nick replied, grinning like an idiot.

'Tara Holdsworth?' Zoe asked, impressed he'd even gotten up the guts to ask her.

Jack ruffled Nick's hair and then Molly wanted to know the ins and outs of Nick's outfit and the dance he had to do. It was amazing to see how far Nick had come the last five years from the gangly kid who couldn't get out of his own way to being so close to finishing his apprenticeship. Zoe was proud of him, and like Jack said, it'd be a damn shame to lose him if they couldn't get more steady work.

Chapter 9

Georgia was up early the next morning, and after plotting her day out over a double-shot skim-milk latte and an omelette, she headed off in search of ideas from surrounding hinterland towns to help sell the cottage when it was finished.

She asked about boots when she ordered her breakfast and was informed she'd need to go to the outfitters in town which, as she expected, didn't open until Monday morning. That meant she wouldn't get to be on the job site until after the builders had started. That wasn't optimal but Ren and Rick had assured her the builders knew what they were doing.

She spent the rest of the day driving around winding roads, popping into towns along the hinterland tourist trail, dropping into boutique wineries and walking along main streets with hundred-year-old buildings housing art galleries and specialty food shops. As Ren had predicted, there was a lot of potential to turn the cottage into a bed and breakfast, especially one that utilised locally sourced products.

By the time she arrived back in Elizabeth Creek, it was almost dark and she nearly tripped over the old pair of boots sitting on the doorstep of her motel room. At first she thought she'd gone to the wrong door, but on double-checking the number, discovered that it was, in fact, her room. There was a note tucked into the shoelaces of one of the boots. She pulled it out, hoping it might shed some light on the shoes' owner. *'Meet out front, 7am'* was all it said.

She looked around at the empty car park, expecting some burly old worker to wander over, shoeless, having left them at the wrong door and possibly going to miss his ride in the morning.

Then she panicked and thought that perhaps someone had broken into her room and was waiting for her to return. Or perhaps her room had been double-booked. That was the more likely scenario.

Georgia had heard of that happening to friends before, friends who'd been given an upgraded room in return for the inconvenience. She wasn't sure there was such a thing as an upgraded room at a place like the Elizabeth Creek Country Motel, but there was only one thing for it. She'd have to go and talk to reception and get the problem sorted out.

The bell on the door at reception tinkled as she entered and the manager behind the desk smiled when she looked up. 'Hi. What can I do for you?'

'I'm Georgia Ballantyne, from room 18. I just wanted to ask, has my room been double-booked?'

The manager shook her head. 'Not that I know of. Why?'

'There's a pair of work boots sitting on the mat outside my door. They obviously belong to someone, and that someone is definitely not me.'

The manager looked confused for a moment while she tapped away on the keyboard and scrutinised whatever it was she was looking at on her computer screen. Then a smile spread across her face. 'Those were dropped off for you,' she said.

'For me?'

'Zoe Jennings dropped them 'round earlier but you weren't here, so she just left them outside your room. Apparently you needed a pair?'

'Are you sure?'

The manager nodded. 'I'm sure. Carol, the day manager, left a note on your booking.'

'Oh. Right.' Georgia wasn't sure what to make of this turn of events. She turned to leave and then turned back. 'You wouldn't happen to know where I can get a pair of socks before tomorrow morning, would you?'

'The outfitters doesn't open 'til nine tomorrow,' the manager replied. 'But there's a lost property box in the laundry you could try. People are always leaving stuff in their rooms and that's where we put it before we donate it.'

'Thanks,' Georgia nodded, heading to the laundry room. The thought of wearing someone else's socks made her feel slightly ill, but the thought of wearing someone else's boots without socks was much worse. If she did happen to find a pair of socks in the lost property, at least she'd be able to wash them before she wore them.

Chapter 10

The first day of a new job was always exciting, at least for Nick, which was why he was sitting outside the work shed waiting just after 6.30am. For Zoe, first days, and first weeks, were always fraught with danger, especially for renovation jobs. You never knew what you had until you started pulling a house apart. The fact they hadn't done a big job like this one for a while was also playing on her mind. She hoped Jack had the timings right and had to trust he'd ordered everything that needed to be ordered.

'I haven't even had my coffee yet,' Zoe grumbled as she unlocked the gate and went inside. Nick followed her in and closed the gate behind them.

'Demo day,' he said. 'Best day of the build.'

'Only because you don't get into trouble for smashing things,' Zoe replied. 'Get my Cruiser loaded up while I make sure we've got the right plans.' As

Nick hurried off into the shed, she called, 'Load up the other one too. You can take that one today with the trailer. I have to pick up Georgia this morning so I'll meet you up there.'

Nick grinned. 'Righto, Boss.'

She resisted the urge to admonish him for calling her 'boss', something she hated, but she let him go. He was like a kid in a lolly shop in the early stages of a build. Hopefully she could keep his attention until the end of this one. He waned a bit as it got into the nitty gritty. He was impatient to get things finished and although he was getting better, he still tried to cut corners sometimes when she wasn't paying attention, just to get jobs done.

Zoe unlocked the office door and flicked through the plans on Jack's desk until she found the ones for Carramar. These were the plans that would stay on site for the plumber and electrician to use when they came in to do their bit in a couple of weeks' time.

They'd already been sent through to all the sub-contractors, but there was always someone who forgot to bring theirs. She rolled them up and shoved them into a tube, tucked it under her arm and went back outside where Nick was finishing up.

'Ready to go,' Nick said, wiping his hands on his jeans.

'I shouldn't be too far behind you. Just get all the tools out ready and we'll get started as soon as I get there.'

Nick saluted and jumped into his ute and drove off. Too late, Zoe realised he'd left the drinks esky behind. She shook her head and hoisted it up onto the back of her ute. 'One day he'll get it right,' she muttered. She jumped into her ute and headed for the motel to pick up Georgia, with a quick stop at the cafe on the way.

She was surprised to see Georgia was waiting out the front of the motel when she arrived, and even more surprised to see she was wearing the boots she'd dropped off the day before. They looked out of place against the tight jeans and long-sleeved linen shirt Georgia was wearing, but she was dressed better than Zoe expected. At least the linen shirt would keep Georgia cool.

Georgia opened the passenger's side door and got in. 'Thanks for the boots,' was the first thing she said.

'You wouldn't get any your size at the outfitters,' Zoe said. 'It'd take at least a week to get them in.' She handed Georgia a coffee. 'Double-shot skim milk latte,' Zoe said. 'BJ said that's what you ordered yesterday.'

'Thanks,' Georgia replied, accepting the coffee and taking a sip. 'Much better than the instant they have in the motel room.'

Georgia was a lot perkier than Zoe thought she'd be this early in the morning. A lot of people said they liked to get up early, but not many were actually telling the truth.

They drove in amicable silence, each happy to drink their coffee, listening to the staticky morning radio until they got to the house. The roadwork crew weren't due for another hour or two, depending on when Rowan got his butt out of bed and into work, so the road in was still rough. By the time they pulled up at the back of the cottage, Nick had shown some initiative and had started setting the tools up in one of the old machinery sheds.

As she pulled her ute up next to his, he pulled the last of the tool boxes from the tray and set it down beside the saw horses.

He'd also set up the plan easel next to the car, ready for Zoe to tack the printed plans to. They could stay in the shed for the moment, at least until they got the demo done inside.

Zoe directed Georgia to the back of the ute. 'If you're going to hang around here all day, you may as well help out.'

Georgia smiled. 'Sure. What do you need me to do?'

'There's a couple of eskies here with drinks and plates and stuff, and Nick's got some chairs and tables in the back of his ute. You could find somewhere out of the way to set them up so we've got a place to have our breaks.'

She pulled the heaviest of the eskies off the ute and placed it on the ground.

'You want me to look after the food?' Georgia asked.

'Yes,' Zoe replied. She grabbed her hard hat from the back of the ute and pulled it onto her head. 'There's an urn in one of the boxes. You should make sure that gets filled up from the tank here and plugged in straight away. The boys drink coffee like it's water.'

She picked up a sledgehammer and a crowbar and headed for the cottage, hoping Georgia would be kept busy enough with the food to stay out of their way.

Chapter 11

'Lunch lady,' Georgia muttered to herself as she set up the folding table in the old shed behind the cottage. 'That's how she wants me to help out.' She shook her head. 'I bet she's expecting me to make their damn coffees too.'

She thrust a fold-up chair in front of her and set it down beside the table. She did that with three more chairs and then opened up the lid on one of the eskies. It was full of soft drink and water and in the corner was a bottle of milk.

She opened a storage box to discover melamine plates and cups and a small hot water urn. She pulled it out and set it on one of the tables and held the power cord, wondering where on earth she was meant to plug it in.

'Simmo will be here soon,' Nick said as he placed another box on the ground. 'He's the sparky. He'll set you up with power. There's a sandwich maker in there too, if you wanted to have a toastie for lunch. I'll catch ya later.' He picked up a crowbar and walked over to the cottage.

Georgia let out a huff and started unpacking the coffee tins and other containers. Once she was done, and since the electrician still hadn't arrived, she looked around for something else to do. She wasn't going to let Zoe relegate her to running after the rest of them with drinks and sandwiches all day.

This was her cottage and she intended on working on it.

She spotted a sledgehammer on the ground near the eskies. She picked it up, realising it was heavier than it looked, and then considered her options.

The banging and crashing inside the house had started and Georgia looked at the outdoor toilet. A smile spread across her face. She'd show Zoe a thing or two about what she could do with a hammer.

She slung the sledgehammer over her shoulder, stomped over to the old toilet and sized up her target. She picked a spot on the wall and swung hard. The timber cracked but it barely made an impact. Georgia glanced over at the house, wondering if her demolition efforts would be heard inside. Probably not, she figured, judging by the sound of the banging and crashing going on in there.

She lined up another spot on the wall and swung with all she could muster. There was another satisfying crack and this time, the old toilet wobbled. Georgia was surprised at how good she felt, swinging a sledgehammer at a timber wall. No wonder all those renovation show TV hosts got excited by 'demo day'.

Another hit in the same spot splintered the timber, making a hole and Georgia felt strangely euphoric. She took a moment to rethink her tactics. Trying to bring the old toilet down by hitting each timber board obviously wasn't working. Maybe if she tried hitting the corners that might work.

She adjusted her stance, drew back the sledgehammer and swung with everything she had.

* * *

The kitchen was almost completely down when there was a crash outside and then a scream.

Zoe and Nick both dropped their tools and raced down the back steps to find the old outdoor toilet in splinters all over the ground.

Zoe cast her eyes around for Georgia, at first thinking she'd managed to bury herself in the rubble but saw her standing on the back of Nick's ute.

'What the hell is going on?' Zoe demanded, stomping across the yard to the ute. 'What the—'

'Snake,' Georgia said, pointing a shaky finger at the remnants of the outdoor toilet.

'Aw, it's a big old python,' Nick cooed.

Zoe walked back over to have a look. In the middle of the remains lay a mass of writhing green and brown scales.

'Poor thing was probably having a good old snooze,' Nick said, pulling away debris.

Zoe started pulling bits of timber away from the snake and said to Nick, 'Go get a couple of shovels and the bin from inside.'

Nick hurried off back into the house.

'You're not going to kill it, are you?' Georgia called from the ute.

'Of course not,' Zoe replied. 'We're going to relocate it to somewhere much safer.'

'Thank you,' Georgia said.

'I meant for it, not for you,' Zoe sniped.

Nick returned and handed Zoe a shovel and together they proceeded to probe and prod the python until it decided the bin was the safest place for it.

They popped the lid on top and then together, carried it to the back of the shed, where they upended it and stepped back, watching the snake slither away into the grass.

Zoe had no doubt it would be back soon enough, but she wouldn't tell Georgia that. She sent Nick back into the house with the bin and told him to finish pulling down the kitchen.

She walked back to the front of the shed and found Georgia sitting on a folding chair, looking sheepish.

'What the hell do you think you're doing?' Zoe asked. 'If you can't stay out of trouble, I'm taking you back into town.'

'I didn't realise it would come down like that,' Georgia replied.

'That's why I'm the builder,' Zoe said. 'Leave the building to me.'

Georgia stood up. 'And what am I meant to do? Be your damn lunch lady?'

'I told you you didn't have to be here for the demo but no, you just had to come. There's nothing for you to do today,' Zoe said.

'I'm quite capable of helping,' Georgia replied. She crossed her arms across her chest, defiant.

Zoe glanced across to the old outdoor toilet, now a crumpled mess on the ground. She shook her head. 'Just stay out of my way.' She stomped off back toward the house.

'Don't treat me like an idiot,' Georgia yelled to her back.

'Then stop acting like one,' Zoe yelled over her shoulder.

Damn clients, she thought. She knew it would be a bad idea to have Georgia on site for the first few days but Jack had to insist. As soon as they broke for lunch, Nick was taking Georgia back into town, and she could stay there where she wouldn't cause any more trouble.

Chapter 12

Demolishing the old outdoor toilet and inadvertently discovering a snake was probably not the smartest thing Georgia had ever done, and it had almost been enough to make her want to go back to town, but she was determined to show Zoe she wasn't a wuss.

She could've called Ren to have a whinge but decided to wait until she got back to the motel later that night to complain about Zoe. She was sure the lunch lady/demolishing the toilet events wouldn't be the only things she'd be telling Ren that night. The day was still young. Instead, Georgia contented herself with arranging the coffee mugs onto the fold-up table, and mumbling to herself about Zoe being a pain in the arse.

Nick's voice startled her. 'Excuse me, Mrs Ballantyne?'

Georgia spun around. 'I'm not married.'

'Oh, sorry,' Nick replied, looking down at his feet.

'It's okay. Georgia's fine, anyway,' Georgia replied, feeling immediately sorry for being grumpy with Nick. Her beef with Zoe had nothing to do with him.

'Okay, thanks,' Nick replied. 'I just came to tell you that Zoe wants you to come back into town with me.'

Georgia huffed out a breath. 'She's sending me home like a naughty school girl?'

'I have to grab a few things from the shed, and then we have to do the lunch run,' Nick replied apologetically.

'What about all the stuff I just set up?' Georgia asked. 'I thought that was for lunch.'

'Simmo and his boys bring their own so it's mostly for them,' Nick said. 'The boss buys lunch on the first day of a job. It's tradition.'

'Isn't she generous,' Georgia muttered under her breath.

'She also said I need to drop you off at Leroy's to get some boots,' Nick said.

As Georgia followed Nick to the ute, she asked, 'So am I allowed back after you get lunch?'

Nick looked at her over the tray. 'She didn't say you weren't.' He got into the driver's side and started the car.

Georgia glanced back at the cottage where the banging had gotten noticeably louder. Fine. She'd go into town with Nick and order her damn boots. And while she was there, she'd ring Ren and see if there was any way they could get another builder. There was no way Georgia was going to put up with Zoe Jennings for the next four weeks.

* * *

After trying on eight pairs of steel capped work boots, all of them uncomfortable in their own way, Georgia finally settled on a pair and ordered them. She was assured they'd get more comfortable the more they were worn in, but Georgia doubted that, especially since she'd only be wearing them for a few weeks.

After an hour wandering the main street waiting for Nick to finish at the work shed, Georgia met him at the local takeaway to order lunch.

Nick insisted on paying for Georgia's lunch on the work account, telling her it was what they normally did on a build, so Georgia didn't argue.

She wanted to tell Nick that technically, since she was paying the bills, she was the one paying for lunch, but that was semantics and she was sure it would go over Nick's head.

She listened to Nick's advice about lunch though, and took a chance on what he called the best steak burger in town, and watched as he piled burgers, chips and a bag of battered fish and Chiko rolls into a thermal lunch box.

Just as they were heading off, Nick's phone rang. 'Hey Boss,' he said when he answered. 'On our way now.' He glanced over at Georgia. 'Yep, got them all sorted.'

Georgia resisted the urge to roll her eyes. She couldn't believe Zoe was checking up on her.

'No lettuce and double cheese,' Nick said, and he did roll his eyes.

Georgia couldn't resist a chuckle. Sounds like Zoe drove Nick nuts too.

Nick hung up from the call and shoved the phone onto the dash.

Georgia said, 'Has Zoe always been so…'

'Blunt?' Nick finished.

'I was going to say painful,' Georgia replied.

Nick snorted. 'She says what she means which is good, you know. Especially for a boss.'

'If you say so,' Georgia mumbled and looked out the window as they drove back to the cottage.

Chapter 13

Nick and Georgia still hadn't returned with lunch by the time Zoe had finished the demo inside the cottage. She was waiting on Nick to help her demolish the back wall ready for the extension, so she decided to take a break and have a chat to Simmo while she had a coffee.

When she went to put hot water in her mug, Simmo said, 'It's not hot yet. I had to fill it up so it hasn't had time to heat up.'

Zoe thumped her mug down on the table. If this was the way Georgia intended to help, by not doing what she was told, she could go right back off to the city where she came from.

As she sat and waited for the urn to heat up and chatted to Simmo about the build, her phone rang. It was Jack.

'You're causing me some bloody grief, Zoe,' Jack said when she answered.

'What else is new?' Zoe joked, leaning back into the camp chair.

'I got another call from Rick Wheeler—'

Zoe rolled her eyes. 'What the hell am I supposed to have done now?'

'Apparently, you asked Georgia to make the coffees,' Jack said, and before Zoe could cut in he added, 'Now look, it's your work site, I know that, and that's what I said to Rick. But come on, Zo, you have to stop treating Georgia like she's a prickle in your thong.'

'Well that's exactly what she is,' Zoe replied. 'And anyway, she demoed the outback dunny.'

'Really?'

'Yep. Didn't even wait to be asked to,' Zoe said and she hoped Jack could hear the sarcasm through the phone.

Jack let out a breath and Zoe could take a guess that he was doing that thing where he squished his face like he looked like he was in pain. 'Where is she now?'

'In town getting the lunches with Nick,' Zoe replied.

'You sent her to get the lunch? No wonder she got upset.'

'I sent her back into town to get some boots,' Zoe replied. The fact that she got two good hours without Georgia Pain-in-the-arse was a bonus. She didn't say that to Jack.

'Look, can you just find her something to do there? Expanding this business depends on you doing a bloody good job on that cottage.'

Zoe saw the tell-tale dust plumes from an approaching vehicle. A truck pulled up in front of the house and Nick's ute drove around behind and pulled up near the shed. 'Nick's back with lunch and the load of chamfer's just arrived. I have to go.'

'Just promise me I won't be getting any more angry phone calls from Rick Wheeler,' Jack said.

'You know I hate to make promises, Jack. I'll see you later.'

She hung up the phone, and as the driver got out of the truck carrying the reclaimed chamfer board that would be used on the exterior of the extension, she knew exactly what she could get Georgia to do to keep her out of trouble.

'I wonder how helpful she'll want to be when she's pulling nails out of timber all day,' Zoe muttered to herself as she headed over to the ute to get her lunch.

Chapter 14

Georgia could've sworn the pile of wood was getting bigger. She double checked the board she was working on was free of nails and then placed it onto the pile to her right. She picked up another one from the pile on her left, put it down on the saw horses and got to work pulling out the nails.

She'd been at this job for nearly three hours, and she'd only seen Zoe once in that time, which was fine by her.

As much as the work was repetitive and boring, she wasn't going to let a builder on a power trip get the better of her. Besides, it was a good way to work out her frustrations, and to get her hands dirty. It had been way too long since she'd done anything remotely like physical labour, and she was surprised to find that she was enjoying the feeling of accomplishment at seeing the pile on her left grow smaller as the pile on her right grew bigger.

Getting a client a good deal on a mortgage just didn't hold the same sort of sense of accomplishment, she realised.

She tossed another newly nail-less board onto the pile and wiped her forehead with the back of her hand.

Simmo appeared in the doorway to the shed. 'You might want to come and see this. The back of the old house is going down.'

'Thanks,' Georgia replied and stood up, stretching out her hands. She put her hammer down and walked outside. She squinted into the sunshine until her eyes adjusted and then walked over and stood beside Simmo, far enough away from the house to not be in the way. She pulled off her gloves and took her phone from her pocket ready to take some photos.

Simmo pointed to the house. 'They've cut right through the brick and posts all the way 'round, so they'll just push it over.'

'Won't the roof come down?' Georgia asked, her phone poised, ready.

'The brick's not load-bearing,' Simmo explained. 'And they've shored it up inside. It'll be fine.'

There was a yell from inside the house and then the brick wall began rocking back and forth before it finally came down with a massive crash, throwing dust and debris into the air. When the dust cleared, Zoe and Nick were standing at the back of the house, now open to the elements, grinning. They high-fived each other and then Zoe slapped Nick on the back. Georgia found it hard to not grin herself. Seeing the back wall come down like that was oddly satisfying. She locked eyes with Zoe and for a second they held each other's gaze before Zoe broke it off and turned and walked back into what remained of the cottage.

Nick and the other builders started removing the debris and tossing it into wheelbarrows and carting it to the skip bin at the front of the house.

Simmo headed to the pile of rubble. 'Come on. Last job for the day. Sooner we get this in the bin, the sooner we knock off.'

Georgia shoved her phone into her pocket, pulled her gloves back on and started picking up bricks and other debris and tossing them into wheelbarrows. At least it would be a break from pulling nails.

* * *

After a couple of hours, Nick and Georgia finally tossed the last of what remained of the back wall into the skip, and Zoe decided to call time for the day. Georgia walked back over to the shed and began packing up the eskies, mugs and plates.

'Just the eskies,' Nick said, appearing beside her, clipping the lid down on one of them before picking it up and carrying it to his ute. 'We're all coming back tomorrow so all that other stuff can stay here.'

'You might be coming back tomorrow,' Georgia replied. 'But I'm not so sure your boss will let me back.'

Nick waved his hand like he was swatting at a fly. 'Nah, it's all good. She's just antsy on the first day of a job. She'll be better tomorrow.'

Georgia very much doubted that. She helped Nick lift another esky onto the back of his ute.

'Are you coming to the pub later?' he asked.

'I think I'll just head back to the motel and grab a takeaway or something,' Georgia replied.

'That's a bit boring. Plus,' Nick said, nodding over to where Zoe was talking to Simmo. 'The boss shouts the first round of drinks after the first day on a new job. Can't say no to a free beer, can ya?'

'Are you sure she won't mind? I'm not exactly one of the workers,' Georgia said, glancing at Zoe. She wasn't sure she wanted to spend any more time together after the day they'd had.

'She'll be right,' Nick said. 'Besides, where else are you going to eat on a Monday night? There's not much to choose from outside of the weekends.'

'Fair enough,' Georgia replied. 'I guess I'll eat at the pub.'

Nick closed the side of the ute tray and flipped the lock. 'See you there,' he said with a grin.

Georgia looked over to where Zoe was gesticulating to Simmo, probably going over the next day's plans. 'Actually, Nick, do you mind if I go back into town with you? I want to have a shower and get changed before I get dinner. It looks like Zoe might not be ready to go just yet.'

'Yep, sure,' Nick replied. 'Jump in.'

He reversed the ute around closer to Zoe. 'Hey boss. I'm off. Georgia's coming back to town with me.'

Zoe glanced at Georgia and nodded at Nick. 'Righto.'

'Your shout at the pub?' Nick asked.

Zoe shook her head but smiled. 'Only if you've cleaned out the eskies and got everything ready to go for tomorrow by time I get back to the shed.'

Nick mock-saluted his boss and drove off.

'Hey, ah, you mind giving me a hand back at the shed?' Nick asked. 'It'll get us to the pub sooner.'

Georgia smiled and nodded. 'Sure. Why not?' It wasn't like she had anything better to do. And at least Nick asked nicely, unlike a certain someone who was disappearing in Georgia's side mirror as they drove off.

Chapter 15

Nick sunk the eight ball on the pool table and blew the tip of the pool cue. 'Two all,' he said. 'Next one wins?'

Bloody show off, Zoe thought, shaking her head. 'Rack'em up again,' she said, chalking up her cue. 'And this time, if you bump the table, I'm taking two shots.'

Nick grinned and drank his beer. 'You still won't beat me.'

'Whatever you say, lightweight,' Zoe replied. After a trying day, she was onto her second beer, and she finally felt relaxed. The first day on a job like the cottage renovation was always the worst for Zoe. No matter how well everything was planned, something always popped up to derail the schedule. This time, though, the demolition hadn't thrown up anything unexpected, which was a nice change.

The only spanner in the works had been Georgia Ballantyne. Zoe shook her head at the thought of having to spend another three and a half weeks with her.

She was glad she'd found Georgia a job that kept her busy and out of her hair for the afternoon. There was enough timber to keep her busy pulling nails for the next couple of days, especially if she got her to sand them back too.

She wondered whether she should tell Georgia about the sanding tomorrow, or wait until she finished pulling the nails. Maybe she should wait until she finished the nails. That was the painful job, and Nick would be glad to not have to finish that one. Zoe was certain that once Georgia found out she'd be sanding all those pieces of timber too, she'd give up and stay in town and let the rest of them get on with the job.

Zoe leaned in low over the pool table, lining up her shot to break in the next game against Nick. As she played her shot, there was a low whistle from someone sitting nearby. Zoe stood up and looked over to the door where everyone's gaze seemed to be centred.

Georgia Ballantyne stood in the doorway in tight-fitting jeans and a loose button down shirt, her hair looking freshly done. Those jeans were definitely unsuitable for the work site. No room for anything in those pockets.

'What's she doing here?' Zoe grumbled.

'I asked her,' Nick said, shoving Zoe out of the way so he could have his shot. He potted a ball and then had a second shot. When he was finished, he waved at Georgia to get her attention.

Georgia smiled and waved back and walked over and placed her purse on their table.

'Have I missed the first round shout?' Georgia asked.

'Yeah but I'm sure the boss won't mind getting you one anyway,' Nick replied. 'Hey boss?'

Zoe wanted to clip him over the ear for his audacity, but instead said, 'Go grab a drink and tell Robbo it's on me.'

'Thanks,' Georgia replied and turned and walked over to the bar.

Zoe couldn't help but notice how Georgia's jeans showed off her butt. She shook her head. What was she thinking, checking out her client's butt like that?

'She's way out of your league,' Simmo said from behind her.

'She's not even in a league I want to play in,' Zoe replied.

'Hey, boss,' Nick called.

Zoe turned and glared at him. 'What?'

He grinned at her, totally ignoring the annoyed tone in her voice, and said, 'Your shot.'

Zoe finished her beer and held up the glass to Nick. 'Your shout, rookie.'

Nick rested his pool cue against the wall and walked around the pool table. He took Zoe's empty glass and she said, 'Last drinks. We've got another big day tomorrow.'

Nick nodded and headed to the bar. As he passed Georgia, who was heading back to the group, he leaned in and said something. Georgia nodded, looked over to Zoe and smiled. What was that little shit up to?

Zoe stood up, had her pool shot and sat down to wait for Nick to get back.

Georgia returned from the bar, placed her beer on a coaster and sat on a stool.

'I didn't take you for a beer drinker,' Zoe said.

'I don't mind one now and then,' Georgia replied. 'Besides, I didn't want to have anything too expensive, since you were paying for it.'

She thinks I'm a bloody cheapskate, Zoe thought. 'What do you normally drink?' Zoe asked.

'Red wine,' Georgia replied. 'Or a scotch.'

'I don't mind a scotch and coke every now and then,' Zoe said.

'I prefer mine neat,' Georgia said. She took a sip of her beer and placed it down. 'It tastes better over ice.'

Snob, Zoe thought. Nick returned with her beer and saved her from having to make any more small talk. 'Your shot,' she said.

Nick potted two more balls and pulled his bar stool over to the table and planted himself next to Georgia. As Zoe leaned over the pool table to have her shot, she overheard Nick say, 'See? Told you she was in a better mood than this morning.'

Zoe put more into her shot than she should have and bounced the white ball off the table.

Chapter 16

Georgia wasn't surprised when Zoe informed her she'd have to sand down the chamfer boards after she finished pulling out the nails, and she was sure she detected a hint of self-satisfaction in Zoe's voice. After two-and-a-half days of pulling nails, Georgia guessed she should probably be grateful to not be doing the lunch run or making coffees again.

Getting her hands dirty was proving to be surprisingly therapeutic. It reminded her of the sculpture class she'd taken with Amy and a group of their friends for a hen's party. Of course, true to tradition, they'd had a naked male model, but the laughs she'd shared with Amy over their straight friends getting goo-goo-eyed over him like giddy school girls was worth it. And the sight of their jaws dropping when his boyfriend turned up to pick him up after class was priceless.

She closed her eyes and swallowed hard, took a deep breath and let it out again. Memories of Amy had become a dull ache over the last few years, and the fact that the cottage seemed to be bringing them up again made her realise she'd made the right decision to sell it and move on.

'Georgia?' Nick wandered into the shed, his hands in his pockets. Why did he always look scared of approaching her? She wasn't scary, was she?

'Hey, Nick. What's up?'

'We've taken the old cast iron tub out of the bathroom and Zoe said to ask you if you'd decided what to do with it yet?'

Just great. Zoe couldn't even be mature enough to come and ask questions herself now.

'I haven't really thought about it to be honest,' Georgia admitted. 'What do you think?'

'Me?' Nick said. 'I dunno. It's your bathroom.'

'I know,' Georgia replied. 'But you're a builder, right?'

'Apprentice,' Nick corrected her.

'Right,' Georgia said. 'So if this was your house, what would you do? Would you keep it or put in a new one?'

Nick ran his fingers through his hair and blew out a breath. 'Well, I'd probably keep it I reckon. Resurface it, obviously, but I think I'd keep it.'

'Would you? You wouldn't want a brand new bath?' Georgia asked.

'New ones are all the same,' Nick said, scratching his chin. 'Cast iron ones, at least in this condition, are hard to find. You shouldn't throw it out, anyway. It's probably worth a bit of money. You could maybe sell it if you didn't want it.'

Georgia nodded thoughtfully. 'Thanks, Nick. Can I have a think about it?'

'Yep. Just let me know when you decide.' He turned and walked out, leaving Georgia with her thoughts. She'd talk to Ren about the tub when she called her. She wasn't confident on making design calls so early, especially since she hadn't seen the final details from the designer yet. How could she know if she wanted to keep the old bath tub if she didn't even know whether it would fit in the new bathroom?

She pulled on her dust mask, turned on the sander and started on the next board. It was a messy job but at least it was better than pulling nails.

Chapter 17

Zoe answered her phone before she realised who it was. When she heard Frank Dickson's voice on the other end, she had to resist just hanging up on him and blaming it on the network.

'What do you want, Frank?' she asked instead.

'I just wanted to make sure you were on track with your move,' Frank replied, as cheery as if he was having an everyday conversation. As if what he'd done to Zoe hadn't affected her future. She had big plans for that old workshop and now they were in tatters.

'I'm working, Frank,' Zoe replied.

'Look, Zoe, you need to be out of there in three weeks. I don't want to have to forcibly—'

'Jesus, Frank. I've just started a new project. Like you said, I've got three more weeks to move. Get off my damn back.' And with that she hung up on him. It was almost knock-off time and it was the end of the week, so rather than get started on something else, she told her crew to take an early mark. Then she wandered down to the big shed where she'd set Georgia up in the far corner to sand the chamfer boards.

The back extension was ahead of schedule with the roof due to be finished on Monday, and although she didn't want to hurry Georgia along, it would be good to see if they had enough chamfer to start the external walls. Being able to start that job Monday afternoon would mean they'd be ahead of schedule on the build. Apart from that, they were supposed to get some rain next week and it would be good to get the cottage water tight.

The sander was still buzzing when Zoe reached the shed. She leaned against a post and watched as Georgia moved the sander along the board. Her dark hair was pulled back in a loose bun and covered in sanding dust. Her face was covered completely by the dust mask and safety glasses Zoe had given her yesterday.

Zoe was also surprised to see how much Georgia had done. There would be plenty of timber ready to start the external walls. She hated to admit it, but she was impressed. She pushed away from the door frame and walked inside, waiting until Georgia finished the board she was working on before she got her attention.

Georgia jumped a little when Zoe waved a hand in front of her, and took off her ear muffs. 'Are you checking up on me?' Georgia asked.

'Sort of my job, since this is my site,' Zoe replied. She immediately regretted the tone in her voice but didn't apologise. 'I just wanted to see how you were going. It's nearly knock-off time,' she said, trying to keep the annoyance out of her voice this time. Bloody Frank Dickson, getting her in a bad mood.

Georgia took her gloves off and checked her watch. 'Oh, wow. I didn't realise the time.'

'Well anyway, we're starting to pack up, so you should get the tools locked up so we can head back into town.' She turned to walk away.

'Don't you want to check the boards?' Georgia asked.

Zoe detected a hint of sarcasm. She turned around. 'Would it make you feel better if I did?'

'Like you said, you're the boss. Shouldn't you be checking the quality?'

Zoe couldn't work out if Georgia was trying to be a smart arse, or whether it just came naturally. She walked back over to the pile of chamfer and glanced at it. It was then that she realised Georgia had taken them right back to bare timber. She picked up a piece and ran her hands over it. She probably couldn't have done a better job herself.

She placed it back on the pile. 'You didn't need to take it all the way back to bare timber,' she said.

'I'm sorry?' Georgia asked.

'It's getting painted,' Zoe explained. 'You just had to take the top layer of paint off to give us a good surface to paint on.'

Georgia pulled her ear muffs from off her neck and ripped off her dust mask. 'Are you joking?'

Zoe shook her head. 'No. I'm sure I made that clear.'

'You bloody did not,' Georgia snapped. 'Do you think I would've spent all this time on them if I'd known that? I could've had them all finished by now.'

'You've done a lot more than I thought you would,' Zoe said.

'Is that meant to be a compliment?' Georgia asked.

'Sure, if you want,' Zoe said. 'Make sure you bring the sander and the extension cord over and put them in the lock box.' She turned and walked back to the cottage to make sure Nick hadn't missed anything inside.

'Hey, wait a minute,' Georgia called.

Zoe didn't stop walking, but Georgia must have run to catch up with her. She grabbed Zoe by the arm, pulling her around to face her.

'What is wrong with you?' Georgia asked, dropping her hand away.

'Me?' Zoe asked.

'Yes, you. Is it so bloody hard for you to say something nice?'

'You want me to pat you on the head and tell you you've done a good job, is that it?' Zoe asked.

'Would it kill you to say well done?' Georgia replied.

'I don't know,' Zoe snapped. 'Let's see. Well done, Georgia. Happy now?' Her voice dripped with sarcasm, and she resisted the urge to pat Georgia on the head as well, just to make the point. She turned to walk away again.

'No, I'm not happy,' Georgia replied. 'For God's sake can you just stand still and listen for once?'

Zoe should've kept walking. She should've let Georgia have her little hissy fit and then take the weekend to get over it. She should have, but she didn't. Something in Georgia's voice, the frustration rather than the anger maybe, made her stop in her tracks.

She squinted her eyes shut and shook her head. *Just walk away, Zoe,* she told herself, but she couldn't. Instead, she turned around and saw Georgia still standing in the same spot, her hair mussed up and full of white dust. Sanding dust coated her cheeks, a sliver on her nose between where the safety glasses and mask sat, and her forehead, just under her hairline. Her lips were set in a tight line.

'What do you want from me?' Zoe asked, throwing her hands into the air for emphasis.

'For you to be civil,' Georgia replied.

'Have I not been civil?' Zoe asked.

Georgia rolled her eyes and scoffed. 'Is that what you call civil? I'd hate to see when you're being nasty.'

'You have no idea,' Zoe mumbled.

'Look,' Georgia said. 'We've got three more weeks on this build. Can we come to some sort of truce?'

'If that involves you leaving me to get on with the job, sure,' Zoe replied.

'That's not going to happen,' Georgia said. 'I need to work on this project to cut down on labour costs. Can you at least treat me like one of your employees instead of—'

'The pain in the arse you are?' Zoe finished. As soon as the words left her lips, she regretted them, but she didn't take them back. Georgia didn't bite back though. She just narrowed her eyes and glared back.

'I tell you what,' Zoe said. 'I'll do you a deal. I'll treat you just like any other labourer, if you stop running off to Rick Wheeler every time you're angry with me.'

'I'm not angry—' Georgia started to say, but Zoe cut her off with wave of her hand.

'If you've got something to say to me, you say it to me. That's what a labourer would do, right?'

Georgia looked at the ground. 'I suppose so.'

'Good.'

'Shake on it?' Georgia said, sticking out her hand.

Zoe looked at Georgia's outstretched hand. In order to shake it, she'd have to walk over to her, and for some childish reason, she didn't want to be the one to give in. She took a single step forward and stuck out her hand.

Georgia rolled her eyes and took a step forward and as their hands touched, a surge of electricity shot up Zoe's arm. Something must have shown on her face because Georgia cocked her head just slightly as she caught Zoe's eye.

Zoe dropped Georgia's hand and turned away to cover her shock. 'I have to go check that Nick's cleaned up the cottage. Make sure you pack up the sander.'

She didn't know what that was, but the sooner this build was over with, the better.

Chapter 18

After the day she'd had at the cottage, Georgia couldn't wait to get back to her motel room, have a hot shower and wash the dust out of her hair. The confrontation she'd had with Zoe had been coming all week, and while she was glad they'd finally had things out, she wasn't sure anything was actually resolved.

And then there was that feeling she got when she shook Zoe's hand to call a truce. It was like a whole host of fire crackers went off in her arm, tingling all her nerves and sending a shock straight to her heart. She had no idea what that was all about. Maybe it was just the surge of anger and frustration coming out? She wondered if Zoe had felt it too. As she plodded tiredly up the driveway, a familiar voice brought her out of her thoughts.

'Surprise!'

Georgia looked up to see Ren standing in front of her door, arms wide, grinning like an idiot. She walked down to Georgia, who had stopped dead in the middle of the car park too stunned to do anything, and enveloped her in a hug.

'You look like shit,' Ren said, pulling out of the hug and holding Georgia at arm's length.

'Thanks a lot,' Georgia deadpanned. 'What are you doing here?'

'That's a lovely way to greet your best friend,' Ren said, raising an eyebrow.

'You're right. Sorry. I've just had a shit day.'

'Everything okay?' Ren asked.

'I'll be fine,' Georgia replied. 'I just need a hot shower, that's all. How did you manage to get away?'

'I wrangled some 'me time' with Rick so I could come out and see the cottage,' Ren said.

'Where are you staying?' Georgia asked as she opened her door.

'Next door,' Ren replied. She leaned in. 'It's not exactly busy. I just asked if I could have the room next to yours. I think they thought I might've been a stalker or something, the questions they asked me.'

'It's probably more to do with small town gossip,' Georgia said.

'You're probably right,' Ren said. 'Hey, do you reckon they'll think we're having a fling or something?'

Georgia laughed in spite of her mood. 'How have you got so much energy?'

'No kids, remember?' Ren waggled her eyebrows. 'Give me a good night's sleep tonight and I'll have energy to burn on the weekend.'

Inside her room, Georgia dropped into a chair and pulled off her boots. Ren sat on the end of Georgia's bed and looked around.

'This is an exact opposite to my room,' Ren said. She ran her hand over the out-dated flowery bed spread. 'Celia would have a field day in a place like this. Wonder if they'd sell it?'

'You're starting to sound like Rick,' Georgia teased.

Ren ignored the dig. 'So where are you taking me for dinner tonight?' she asked. 'The lady at reception said the pub is the place to be on a Friday night.'

Georgia rubbed her hands over her face and stretched. 'After the day I've had, I just want to stay in. Is that okay?' She was also willing to bet that Zoe Jennings would be at the pub that night too, and after butting heads with her all week, Georgia wanted a couple of days without seeing her at all.

'Sure. How about you have a shower, and I'll go for a wander and bring something back. Then we can have a good catch up and talk about this devil builder of yours.'

'Sure,' Georgia replied. 'Sounds like a plan.'

Ren jumped up off the bed. 'What do you feel like?'

'I don't care. As long as you come back with something alcoholic, I'll eat anything,' Georgia replied.

'You got it,' Ren said. 'I'll see you in a bit.'

Georgia watched Ren leave, closing the door behind her. She hadn't realised how much she missed her best friend right until the moment she saw her outside. Even if it was only for a few days, Georgia was determined to put the last week behind her and enjoy her weekend now that Ren was there.

'I don't know what it is,' Georgia said as she twirled her fork through her noodles, picked some up, blew on them and then popped them in her mouth. 'I just can't do anything right around that bloody woman.' Washing off the day's dust and grime had gone some way to making Georgia feel better. Having Ren surprise her with a visit had also helped.

Ren spooned fried rice onto her plate and mixed it in with her Szechuan beef. 'So she's a perfectionist. Isn't that a good thing for a builder?'

'Maybe,' Georgia conceded. 'But she's doing my bloody head in.'

'Look at the positives. At least you know the cottage is going to look amazing,' Ren said.

Georgia sipped her wine. Unable to find wine glasses in the room, they had to content themselves with coffee mugs. It was either that or drinking straight from the bottle, which Georgia wouldn't have been averse to. 'Yeah, well, at least after this project is finished, I'll never have to see her again.'

'That's the spirit,' Ren replied with a grin.

'Like you said, I'm looking at the positives,' Georgia said, eating another mouthful of noodles. 'Speaking of positives, I never even asked how long you're here for.' If she was here long enough, Ren could see for herself how painful Zoe Jennings was and maybe she could help persuade Rick and Celia to find someone else to finish the build. And if nothing else, having Ren there with her, even if it was just for a few days, would make it much easier to deal with Zoe.

'Aw, I love you too,' Ren grinned.

Georgia pulled a face.

'I'm heading home on Tuesday,' Ren replied.

'That long?' Georgia asked. She was surprised Rick and the kids would be happy to let her go at all, let alone for almost four days.

'That's okay, isn't it? I mean, you haven't got plans for the weekend or anything?' Ren asked.

'No, I haven't,' Georgia replied. 'I can take you for a drive around the hinterland and show you the places I discovered last weekend.'

'Sounds great,' Ren replied. 'There's a liqueur distillery up there somewhere too. Did you find that yet?'

'No, I haven't,' Georgia replied. 'But that sounds amazing.'

'Good, because I've booked us on a tour,' Ren said. She finished the wine in her mug and poured herself another drink. 'I figured the best and easiest way to see the place properly is with people in the know.'

'And you want to drink,' Georgia joked.

'If I'm going to take some me time, I'm going to make the most of it,' Ren replied. 'As long as I bring Rick back a bottle of alcohol of some description and something cheesy for the kids, they won't even care that I've been away.'

'So how are Rick and the kids going to cope without you for that long?' Georgia asked.

'They'll be perfectly fine. And as long as no-one dies, I don't care what they get up to,' Ren said.

Georgia narrowed her eyes. 'Rick's mother is staying, isn't she?'

Ren grinned. 'Yes she is. See why I'm not worrying about them?'

Georgia finished the last of her noodles and sat back in her chair. 'I'm really glad you're here. I can't wait to show you the cottage and talk about what we're doing with the decorating. Actually, speaking of that, Celia hasn't sent any plans through for the inside of the cottage. Has she finished them yet?'

'She's discussed some ideas with Rick, but I think she wants to come see what the cottage looks like once the extension is done before she makes any decisions. Just ask Rick next time you're talking to him.'

'I will,' Georgia replied. 'I've been getting some design questions already. It'd make me feel better if I knew what Celia's intentions were.'

Ren patted Georgia's knee. 'Don't stress. It'll all get sorted, don't worry about it.'

Georgia shook her head. 'I know.' She grinned at her friend. 'I'm really glad you're here.'

Ren grinned back. 'Me too.'

Chapter 19

Zoe pulled open the door to the old workshop and closed it behind her. She turned on the lights, let her eyes adjust to the gloom, and took a deep breath, letting it out slowly. She looked around at the work benches, the piles of timber stacked in neat rows and the tools hanging on the walls. They'd been collected over decades, first by her grandfather, then her father, and Zoe herself had added a few power tools to the old carpentry tools her father had preferred to use.

When she was younger, Zoe hadn't understood her father's preference for the old tools that made repairing or building things take much longer than she thought they had to. Over time, though, she grew to understand that working with wood wasn't meant to be fast. It's why, while building houses and doing renovations was what she did for money, it was here, in this old workshop, that her heart lay. It's where she felt most at home.

She made her way up the steps to the mezzanine floor her father had built before she was born. From here, she could overlook the whole of the workshop. She sat down, letting her legs dangle over the edge, leaning her chin on her hands on the railing, just as she'd done when she was a kid, and closed her eyes. She recalled the image of her father working below, the sloughing sound of the planer on wood filling the silence. The way his leather apron swished as he moved. Him closing one eye as he checked a join, and smiling to himself when he was satisfied with it.

She remembered his huge calloused hands on hers when she was four or five, guiding the planer along a piece of wood, showing her how to be slow and deliberate so she didn't catch it on knots. The ruffle of her hair when he was pleased with her and the click of his tongue when he wasn't.

She wiped away a tear and opened her eyes. In a little over a month, all of this would be gone, leaving an empty shell behind. She still had no idea where she was going to keep all of her equipment, or how she was going to keep the carpentry lessons going. Although the phone call from Frank had been an annoyance, she had to admit that he was right. She needed to work out where she was going to go so she could get the workshop moved out. For now, though, that could wait a little longer. She had doors to find, and window frames to restore for the cottage.

She stood up, shook herself out of her mood and walked over to the old window frames hanging on hooks on the back wall. She pulled them out, one by one, measuring them and discarding the ones that she didn't want on one pile, adding the ones she did want on another.

When she had a pile of six, enough for the cottage extension, she carried them back downstairs and placed them on the bench and got to work.

* * *

Zoe was hand sanding the last window frame when the workshop door squeaked open. She stood up and stretched her back, turning to see who it was. Molly walked over and held out a cotton bag. 'I figured you'd gotten busy.'

'What time is it?' Zoe asked.

'After eight,' Molly replied.

'Shit, Mol. Sorry.' Zoe had been so completely wrapped up in her work that she'd totally lost track of the time.

Molly shook her head. 'It's okay. I thought you might be hungry so I brought you some leftovers.'

Zoe smiled. 'Thanks.'

'It's lasagne,' Molly said. 'Still warm, and there's a fork in there too, in case you needed to finish whatever it is you're doing.'

Zoe pulled the container out of the bag, lifted the lid and breathed in the smell of meat sauce and cheese and herbs. She dug in with the fork and ate a mouthful.

'This is so good, Mol,' she said, chewing. 'I'm so sorry I missed dinner.'

Molly waved her away. 'What's got you so enthralled you forgot the time?'

Zoe had another mouthful of food and pointed to the window frames with her fork. 'I'm prepping some window frames for the cottage.'

'How's that job going?' Molly asked.

'Fine,' Zoe replied, deadpan.

'Is that why Jack's been annoyed with you?' The corner of Molly's mouth twitched up.

Zoe rolled her eyes. 'Georgia's being a pain in the butt is all. I just needed to find something to keep her busy.'

'And away from you?' Molly asked.

'I'm just trying to do my job.'

'Sorry. I wasn't having a go at you,' Molly said. 'I just figured…'

'Just figured what?'

Molly looked around the workshop. 'No-one blames you for being short-tempered at the moment. Losing this place after so long, it must be tough.'

'It's not going anywhere, Molly. Someone's turning it into a bloody brewery.' Zoe finished her mouthful of lasagne, clipped the lid back onto the container and put it and the fork back into the bag. She leaned back onto the bench and crossed her arms.

Molly was giving her one of those sympathetic looks, meaning a hug was probably incoming any second. Molly cocked her head and stepped forward, wrapping her arms around Zoe and squeezing. There it was. Zoe didn't hug her back at first, but finally she pulled her arms from between her and Molly and hugged Molly back. 'I'll be fine.'

Molly nodded against Zoe's shoulder. 'I know you will, Zo. You're always fine.' She pulled away. 'I better get back.'

'Thanks for the lasagne,' Zoe said.

Molly waved her away and disappeared around the door.

Zoe turned back to the work bench, not wanting to think about anything other than her work. She still had a window frame to finish and then she had to prep for tomorrow's woodwork class.

Chapter 20

'Do we even know who Leroy is?' Ren asked as she picked through a rack of long-sleeved work shirts.

'I don't think he's a person,' Georgia replied. Why Ren was fascinated about the owner of Leroy's Outfitters was a mystery.

'It's always a person,' Ren said. 'Probably the guy who started the shop.'

'Why does it matter?' Georgia asked. She looked through a pile of women's jeans, trying to find something appropriate for the work site. There wasn't much choice.

'Small towns,' Ren shrugged. 'That stuff is always important. This guy, Leroy, could've been a very important man around town. You should know this stuff, George.'

Georgia looked over to Ren and shook her head. If Ren ever lived in a small town like Elizabeth Creek, she'd be one of those old biddies gossiping over the back fence. 'I'm going to try these on,' she said.

Ren handed her some long-sleeved shirts. 'Try these on too.'

Georgia looked at the flannelette shirts piled on top of the very blue blue jeans she'd picked. At least she'd finally blend in with the locals. As she carried the pile of clothes to the changing rooms, a boy, about ten, pushed past her and raced over to the wall of Akubra hats. That was where she was putting her foot down. She was happy enough to buy jeans and flannelette shirts, but there was no way she was getting an Akubra. That was a step too far.

She closed the dressing room door behind her and hung up her clothes and began trying them on. The first pair of jeans just didn't feel right at all, so she ditched them and put on the second. She considered herself in the mirror, turning to check out her bum. Not bad. She took off her top and pulled on a red and blue checked flannelette shirt, rolling the sleeves so they sat just above her wrists.

Well, if Zoe wasn't happy with her wearing this at the cottage while she worked, she didn't know what she was supposed to wear. She opened the door to the changing room and backed out, still regarding herself in the mirror.

'Hey, how's this look?' she asked, smoothing her hands over her bum and turning her head from one side to the other.

'They look pretty good to me,' replied a voice that definitely wasn't Ren's.

Georgia spun around to see Zoe standing there, still apparently looking down at her butt. She had the audacity to smirk at her as she raised her gaze to meet Georgia's eyes. Georgia's first instinct was to cross her hands over the front of her as if she were naked. 'I thought you were someone else,' she stammered.

'Clearly,' Zoe replied. 'Nice jeans.'

Georgia felt the prickle of embarrassment creeping up her neck. She backed away into the change room.

'Don't you want my opinion?' Zoe asked.

'No, thank you,' Georgia replied. She closed the door and lay her head against it. She could feel the flush of red still in her cheeks.

'Those shirts are good for work,' Zoe said outside the door.

Georgia didn't reply.

'And get a bigger pair in those jeans.'

Georgia flung the door back open. 'Why? Are you saying these are too small?'

'Because they'll give you more room to move. Work pants aren't supposed to be tight. Bend over.'

'What? No!'

Zoe rolled her eyes. 'I'm not trying to be rude, Georgia. If you bend over, you'll see they're too tight. You won't be able to work in them comfortably.'

Georgia narrowed her eyes. 'I don't care.' She slammed the door shut again. Inside the change room, she bent over, just slightly, and realised that Zoe was right. She huffed out a breath.

She hurriedly put on her own clothes and stood back and looked under the door. She couldn't see any boots so she figured she might be safe. She cracked open the door and, not seeing Zoe, opened it fully and stepped out. Ren spun around, an Akubra on her head, a grin on her face. 'Check this out. Cool, right? I think I might get one each for me, Rick and the kids,' she said. Then she spotted the look on Georgia's face. 'Everything okay?'

'Fine,' Georgia said. 'We should get these and get going up to the cottage so I can show you around.'

'You don't want to try on the hats?' Ren asked.

'Nope,' Georgia replied, striding over to the racks to put her jeans back. She begrudgingly bought two pairs of jeans in the larger size and three flannelette shirts in different colours. As she was about to pay, the boy who'd pushed past her earlier appeared beside her, his face pressed against the glass counter.

'Ryan! Will you stand still?' The sound of Zoe's voice from behind her made the blood drain from Georgia's face. Zoe had a son?

'I'm just looking at the pocket knives.'

Georgia tried not to turn around but Ren said brightly, 'I've got a son around the same age. Ten?'

'Eleven,' Zoe replied. 'He's my nephew.'

Georgia wasn't sure why she felt relieved that this kid wasn't Zoe's. Maybe she felt sorry for the poor kid if he'd had Zoe as his mother. She kept her attention on the counter as she waited for her purchases to be rung up.

'Oh, Miss Ballantyne. Your boots have come in,' the man at the counter said. 'I'll just go and get them for you.' He walked off, leaving Georgia stranded for a while longer.

'They're little energiser bunnies, aren't they?' Ren said.

Zoe laughed, something Georgia hadn't heard until then. It sounded surprisingly warm and genuine. 'You're not wrong. This one goes all day and then just drops like a sack of spuds when he finally stops.'

Ren chuckled. 'God, I wish my two were like that.'

'Anyway, we should be going. Come on, Ryan. You can help me in the workshop. See you on Monday, Georgia.'

Georgia closed her eyes and cringed at the mention of her name. There was a whack on her arm.

'Who was that?' Ren asked, leaning on the counter and looking up at Georgia. 'And how do you know her?'

'That was Zoe Jennings,' Georgia replied.

Ren's mouth dropped open. 'That… that was your devil builder?'

'Shh,' Georgia said. 'I'll tell you about it later.' She smiled at the cashier when he came back and placed a shoe box on the counter. He opened the box and pulled one of the boots out, checking it against the screen and then gave her the total price. Georgia couldn't get out of Leroy's fast enough.

Chapter 21

Zoe set Ryan up on one of the work benches with the building blocks he'd been making for the show's woodwork competition. Together, they chose different coloured paint from Zoe's collection of sample pots, and some brushes for Ryan to get started. She knew Molly would be cranky if Ryan turned up at home with paint all over him, but for Zoe, that was what being a kid was all about. At least it used to be for her. That and working in this workshop with her dad. To appease his mother, Zoe had made sure Ryan was wearing an over-sized t-shirt as a painting smock so he didn't get too dirty.

She cast a quick eye over Dallas' dining setting, and noticed she had a piece of timber with four different stains on it sitting nearby. Zoe smiled. She hadn't actually seen Dallas for a week, but the progress she'd made on her project told Zoe she'd been in a couple of times since last Saturday when Zoe had given her the job. She wondered whether Dallas would want to keep this one or sell it, like she did everything else she'd worked on. Maybe she'd enter it into the Elizabeth Creek show this year. Stranger things had happened.

She walked over to the other bench and pulled out the boxes her class had started last weekend. Some of them still had some sanding to do before they chose paint or stain colours, and she figured today she might show them how to use the wood burner to draw designs into their lids. They needed to get them finished today if they were going to enter them into the junior carpentry competition at the show.

As she pulled out the tools and set up for her class, she thought about running into Georgia at Leroy's. It was totally unexpected but not entirely unpleasant. She was pleased Georgia had listened to her advice about getting more appropriate clothes for the work site, though she did hope Georgia went for a better choice of jeans. Tight jeans had no place on a work site.

Georgia had seemed embarrassed to see her but that was possibly because she'd been busted checking out her butt. In Zoe's defence, she hadn't realised it was Georgia's butt she'd been checking out and, she had to admit, it was quite a nice one. She knew it was completely inappropriate to be thinking about her client's backside, especially when that client had been such a pain in Zoe's own arse for the entire last week.

Then there was that other woman with Georgia. Zoe had seen them wandering around in Leroy's, and the way they were interacting, she wondered if they were together. They were definitely close, that was for sure. And then when the woman said she had two kids, that totally threw Zoe. She didn't know what it was about Georgia, but she didn't seem the type to have kids. At least, she hadn't mentioned them, though that was probably not unusual. Georgia Ballantyne seemed to hold her cards close to her chest.

Zoe checked her watch. She had a half hour before her class were due to arrive, so she wandered over to check on Ryan's progress. Painting wooden building blocks might help to keep her mind off of her client's backside.

Chapter 22

'Wow,' Ren said, standing at the front of the yard, looking across the paddocks at the view beyond.

'It's amazing, isn't it? Amy would've loved it.'

Ren turned and smiled. 'Yes, she would have.' She walked over and linked arms with Georgia. 'Show me the cottage and tell me where we're up to.'

Georgia took Ren around the back of the cottage, as that was the easiest way to access it now that it had been opened up. 'This is the new part,' she said. 'All the living areas will be here, as well as the new master suite.' She wandered through the open timber frames and stood where the master ensuite was going to be. 'There's going to be a huge picture window here.'

Ren nodded. 'That's going to be amazing. Tell me there's going to be a big bath tub there to soak in.'

'I have to discuss that with Celia I suppose,' Georgia said, mentally adding it to the list.

Ren wandered in and sat down next to the external wall. 'Can you imagine if you had a big claw foot tub right here with those old fancy taps?' She crossed her legs and lay back as if she were in a tub. 'That's what would sell the place.'

'Do you think so?' Georgia asked.

'Of course. You're going for country luxury, aren't you?'

'I guess so.' Georgia walked out of the ensuite and into the main part of the extension. 'We'll go through the original part of the house and then I want to show you something.'

'Oh? Sounds curious,' Ren said.

'I just want your opinion, that's all.'

'Okay. Lead on,' Ren said, following Georgia around as she explained what they were planning with the original part of the cottage.

After they finished the tour, Georgia took Ren down into the shed and pulled back the tarp covering the old cast iron bath tub.

Ren drew in a breath and she leaned down and ran her hands along the edge of the tub. 'Is that original?'

'I think so,' Georgia replied. 'They want to know if I want to have it resurfaced and put back into the bathroom.'

'You said yes, didn't you?' Ren asked.

'I didn't know what Celia's plans were,' Georgia replied.

'This would be perfect in front of that picture window in the master ensuite,' Ren said.

'You think so?'

'Of course I do,' Ren replied. 'You're nuts if you don't put this back in.'

'What about Celia?'

'Just send her a picture of it and tell her it's going in the ensuite. She'll design everything else around it.'

Georgia nodded. 'Okay. I'll let Zoe know.'

'Speaking of Zoe,' Ren said, her eyes sparkling. 'Why didn't you introduce us at the shop?'

'You can meet her on Monday,' Georgia replied, turning away.

'I met her today,' Ren said. 'Is there something going on I should know about?'

Georgia snorted out a laugh. 'Far from it. You've heard me complaining about her the last week. She just gets on my nerves and I'd rather not see her outside of the build.'

Ren narrowed her eyes but didn't say anything more about it. Instead she said, 'There's one more thing I want to see.'

'What's that?' Georgia asked, glad to change the topic.

'Where you destroyed the outback toilet.'

Georgia rolled her eyes and led Ren back out into the yard.

Chapter 23

After Sunday lunch at Jack and Molly's, Zoe decided she should probably make a start on packing up the old workshop. She knew avoiding it would only make things harder in the end, and when Jack, Molly and the kids offered to help, the decision was made easier. She had to leave enough tools and equipment for her final class before the move, as well as the doors and windows for Carramar, but everything else was going into boxes and ferried to the business shed.

Zoe was hesitant to accept Jack's help initially, but he insisted on storing as much as would fit in the work shed until Zoe found somewhere else to put it all. Ryan and Josie helped as much as they could until Molly took them to her mother's for afternoon tea. That left Zoe alone with Jack, neither of them talking much as they went about their work. Jack packed small tools into boxes while Zoe loaded her ute tray up with piles of timber and ferried them to the workshop.

They'd been at it for a few hours when they decided to break for a drink. When Zoe handed Jack a beer, he said, 'We should toast to something.'

'Like what?' Zoe asked, twisting the cap off her bottle.

Jack held his bottle out. 'How about to Dad?'

'And to all the stuff he built here,' Zoe added.

Jack smiled as they clinked their bottles and had a drink. They drank in amiable silence for a while until Jack said, 'Do you remember the pranks dad used to play on us?'

Zoe smiled and nodded. 'The fake finger he scared us with is still around here somewhere.'

'Is it?' Jack asked, surprised. 'I thought that was lost years ago.

'I found it after he died. I was going to use it on Ryan but I never got around to it.'

Jack laughed into his beer. 'Molly would kill you.'

'I know,' Zoe grinned. She took a long drink of her beer and let out a long breath. 'I thought we'd always have this place.'

Jack nodded. 'I thought you'd end up living here.'

Zoe snorted. 'That was the plan, wasn't it?' She looked up at the mezzanine floor. 'Build that in up there, fireman's pole to get back down, isn't that what we said when we were kids?'

'Dad had a big piece of steel pipe to put up the pole, but Mum wouldn't let him,' Jack said.

'Did he really?' Zoe asked, surprised.

Jack nodded. 'She thought one of us would end up breaking our necks falling down the hole.'

Zoe smiled and shook her head. 'She was probably right.'

'Yeah,' Jack replied. He sucked in a breath and let it out slowly. 'God I miss them.'

'Me too,' Zoe said. She leaned her head on her brother's shoulder. 'Eighteen years.'

Jack nodded. 'Weather's not looking too good Friday night. Are you still going out?'

'Bit of bad weather never stopped me before,' Zoe replied. Spending time by herself on the anniversary of her parents' death was something Zoe had done without exception for the last seventeen years. She knew there was rain predicted for the coming week, with a storm possible by the weekend. If it rained, it would just match her mood.

She drained her beer and stood up. 'No rest for the wicked,' she said.

Jack finished his beer and tossed the empty bottle into the bin. 'I can give you another hour or so and then I'll have to get home.'

'Thanks,' Zoe said, handing him a box. With a resigned sigh, she trudged up the stairs and started ferrying doors and window frames to her ute.

* * *

At a tick over six o'clock, Zoe decided it was finally time to call it quits. She'd been driving timber and tools and equipment from the workshop to the shed for the last few hours on her own, and now, with most of the small stuff gone, all that was really left was the big equipment and workbenches. She'd get Nick and a few of his mates to help out when it came time to move them.

She left Dallas's dining setting in the corner of the workshop along with the pots of stain she was still deciding on. Zoe had also packed up some tools into an old toolbox her dad had made years ago, deciding to give Dallas her own set so she could hopefully keep on working on things in her own time. At least until Zoe got something else worked out.

She switched off the inside lights, pulled the heavy doors closed and locked them up. She had one last trip to unload at the shed and then she'd head home. As she turned the corner onto the main street, she saw Georgia and her friend weaving down the footpath. They looked like they'd had a skin full. The way they clung to each other, stumbling and laughing down the street, made a knot twist in Zoe's stomach.

When she stopped for a red light, she heard her name being called. She turned and looked out her window. The woman with Georgia was waving madly at her, calling out to her. What the hell? Georgia was trying to pull her friend's arm down and cover her mouth with her free hand.

At least one thing was for certain. If Georgia was hungover tomorrow morning, Zoe might get a day at the cottage without her. Why did that thought not make her as happy as she thought she'd be? And why did the thought of Georgia Ballantyne having a partner and kids tie her stomach in knots?

The lights finally turned green and Zoe pulled away. She shook her head. 'Bloody hell, Zoe, what is wrong with you?' she said out loud. She forced her eyes back to the road but as she turned the corner, she couldn't resist a look in her rear vision mirror. Georgia's friend was throwing up in a garden bed while Georgia's eyes were firmly on Zoe as she drove away.

Chapter 24

Georgia wasn't surprised in the slightest when Ren asked for a triple-shot coffee at the cafe on Monday morning and filled it with four teaspoons of sugar, and ordered a bacon and egg roll with double bacon. 'One hangover cure coming up,' said BJ the barista with a grin.

'What makes you think I have a hangover?' Ren asked, squinting as she spoke.

'Caffeine and grease are the first things you crave when you've had a big night,' BJ replied. He pushed a menu across the counter. 'We even call that breakfast The Hangover Cure.'

Georgia glanced at the menu and dug Ren in the ribs.

'You're not the first,' BJ added with a wink and turned to make the coffees.

The graders had finished the road to the cottage, and although she still had to organise the proper roadworks, Georgia could at least take her own car to the cottage and not rely on Zoe. When they pulled up beside the sheds, Georgia was pleased to see the roof of the extension was half completed. It was starting to look like a real house.

'Looks like there's not much we can do,' Ren said heading straight over to the shed where she proceeded to make her second coffee of the day. Things would get interesting once the caffeine kicked in, Georgia thought. She left Ren to recover in the shed and went in search of Zoe. Nick directed her to the roof, where Zoe and another builder were screwing down sheeting. Georgia waved to get Zoe's attention and Zoe nodded in return.

Georgia went around to meet Zoe by the ladder, and when she climbed down, Zoe said, 'Enjoy your sleep in?'

'I did, actually,' Georgia replied. 'Although it wasn't me that needed to stay in bed.'

They both looked across to the shed, where Ren had her coffee mug up to her nose, apparently inhaling her caffeine instead of drinking it.

'She didn't look in good shape last night,' Zoe said.

'Winery tour,' Georgia said. 'One of us was extremely happy to have some time away from their kids and went a little overboard.' She shielded her eyes as she glanced up at the cottage. 'You've got a heap done already this morning.'

'It's amazing how much you can get done when you don't have people riding your arse,' Zoe said.

Georgia glanced at Zoe, expecting that seemingly permanent scowl but instead finding an amused look on her face.

'Very funny,' Georgia replied. 'I came over to see what I can do today. I don't know if you can count on Ren to be much help, but I can maybe get her to do something that's doesn't make her want to throw up.'

'You can undercoat the chamfer,' Zoe said. 'If you want.'

'If I want?' Georgia asked, surprised. 'So I have a choice?'

'Not really,' Zoe replied. 'It's that or go back into town to get the lunches.'

Georgia narrowed her eyes. Was Zoe trying to be funny? 'I'll paint the chamfer,' she said.

'Good,' Zoe replied. 'Nick will show you where the brushes and paint are. Set up in the shed where you were sanding last week so you're out of the sun. It's going to get hot today.'

'Thanks,' Georgia said, unsure why Zoe would be concerned about the heat. And then she remembered that Zoe was the site boss which meant she should be thinking about all of that.

'Oh and ah, those clothes are much more appropriate,' Zoe said as she climbed back up the ladder.

'I'm glad you think so,' Georgia replied. She wasn't sure why, but Zoe's last comment made her smile.

* * *

With the roof completed just after lunch, Zoe informed Georgia that she wanted to start on installing the chamfer on the extension. Ren and Georgia had painted enough of it that they should be able to stay ahead, which meant that the job would go faster.

Ren took a break to grab a bottle of water and when she came back she said, 'I can see why it's so hard to be here every day.'

Georgia followed Ren's gaze to where Zoe was working near the cottage on the drop saw. She'd taken off her shirt and was working in her singlet. 'I don't know what you're talking about,' Georgia said, watching Zoe longer than she probably should have.

Ren glanced at Georgia and dug her in the ribs. 'Here I was thinking when you said the view was good, you meant the scenery.'

Georgia threatened Ren with a fully loaded paint brush. Ren ducked away and giggled.

'You can't tell me your builder isn't hot,' Ren said. She took a long drink of water and pressed the bottle to her forehead.

Georgia turned her attention back to the timber she was painting. 'Is there something you're not telling me?'

'What do you mean?' Ren asked.

'You're straight, remember?' Georgia replied. 'Not to mention married.'

Ren snorted. 'I can appreciate good form when I see it, and that is good form.'

Georgia glanced up again, and Zoe was wiping the sweat from her forehead with the bottom of her singlet, showing off her abs. Zoe looked up at that exact moment and their eyes locked. Even from this distance, Georgia could see Zoe's lips twitch up into a sly smile. Georgia's breath caught in her throat.

'Hey, earth to Georgia,' Ren said, clicking her fingers in front of Georgia's face.

'Huh?' Georgia said, bringing her attention back to Ren, who was grinning at her, eyebrows raised.

'Like I said,' Ren said. 'Can't complain about the view.'

Georgia rolled her eyes and got back to painting.

Moments later, Nick appeared in the doorway. 'Just wanted to let you know that your tub is on its way to the Sunny Coast to get resurfaced. They're not busy so they reckon it'll only take a couple of days.'

'Thanks, Nick,' Georgia said.

'It's going to look smick in that bathroom, hey?'

'It sure is,' Georgia replied.

'Righto. I better get back to it. See ya later.' Nick turned and headed back to the cottage.

'Smick,' Ren said, pulling a face.

Georgia laughed and risked a quick glance back to the cottage where Zoe was nailing the chamfer onto the cottage walls. The sight of her in that singlet, showing off her abs, stirred something in her stomach. She shook it off and got back to painting.

Chapter 25

Zoe wiped her forehead with the back of her hand and looked up at the sky. There were clouds forming to the west, which wasn't surprising judging by the stickiness that hung in the air. A cool change and rain would be a welcome break.

With an hour to go, she and Nick started covering the holes where the windows were due to go with ply. She'd sent the frames she'd refurbished to the glazier that morning and wasn't expecting them back until the end of the week. Without them, the extension was prone to getting wet. Closing them up with ply in the mean time would save them on clean-up if it did rain.

After they'd finished, Zoe sent Nick home. While he got everything sorted back at the work shed, Zoe could clean up on site. She was emptying out the hot water urn when a car pulled up outside the shed. She glanced up to see that it was Georgia. She was surprised that instead of being annoyed at Georgia turning up again right when she was about to head home, Zoe was happy to see her.

'Does the boss know you're finishing early?' Georgia joked as she walked over to the shed and leaned on a post.

'What she doesn't know won't hurt her,' Zoe replied. She placed the urn in the lock box and wiped her hands on her jeans. 'I didn't expect to see you again today. How's Ren?'

'Ren's fine. I doubt she'll be so eager to taste test liqueurs again though.'

Zoe grinned and nodded. 'So, what brings you back out here?'

'I got an email from the interior designer asking for some photos of the progress,' Georgia explained. 'I thought I better do it before I forget.'

'Right,' Zoe said. 'Well, go for your life. I haven't locked up yet. I'll just hang around until you're finished.'

'Thanks,' Georgia replied, and walked to the cottage.

'Actually,' Zoe said, calling after her. 'Can I show you something?'

'Sounds intriguing,' Georgia said.

'Just an idea I had when Nick and I were working inside today,' Zoe explained.

'Okay, sure,' Georgia replied.

Zoe hooked her measuring tape onto her tool belt and followed Georgia to the cottage. For some reason, the argument they'd had last week had made them turn a corner. Maybe they could get through the rest of the build without killing each other after all.

Zoe gave Georgia some space as she wandered around the cottage, taking photos, kicking at the tape marking out the kitchen layout and typing into her phone.

'So,' Georgia said, finally. 'What was this big idea of yours?'

Zoe walked over to the window in the dining room wall. 'What would you think if we opened this up?'

'Like, a bigger window?' Georgia asked.

'Yes, we could do that,' Zoe replied. 'But I don't think a window takes advantage of the view.'

Georgia considered it for a moment. 'It's a little hard to picture with it covered like that.'

'Give me a sec,' Zoe said. She raced outside and grabbed a drill and a ladder and unscrewed the plywood covering the window. 'How's that?'

Georgia's face appeared in the window frame. 'Better.'

Zoe leaned the plywood on the side of the cottage and went back inside. She stood back where the kitchen was mapped out. 'You can't see much from here,' she said.

Georgia backed away from the window and stood beside Zoe. 'I guess.'

Without thinking, Zoe grabbed Georgia by the shoulders and pushed her forward a few steps, closer to the window. 'If we open it up some more, the view will get heaps better.'

Georgia nodded slowly, and moved forward a few more steps. 'And if we open it up with a floor to ceiling window, it will get even better.'

'Or,' Zoe said, glad that Georgia was getting what she was talking about. 'What about, and this is something you'd have to talk to the designer about, but we could do French doors.' She glanced sideways at Georgia, who cocked her head and then turned and looked at Zoe, a smile playing on her lips.

'Could we do that? Put in doors instead of a window?' Georgia asked.

'Sure,' Zoe shrugged. 'While we're still at the frame stage, anything's possible. Like I said though, any changes like that will add a few days to the end date.'

'I actually think that would be amazing,' Georgia said. 'But we'd have to put a veranda or something out there, wouldn't we??'

'That would be the idea,' Zoe confirmed. 'That would create a whole extra living area.'

'Would it add much to the budget?' Georgia asked.

'Not much,' Zoe replied. 'We already have most of the materials and we've got plenty of reclaimed wood at the shed.'

'Okay,' Georgia said. 'Would we need to get permission from council? If it's going to get held up there then it might not be worth it.'

'Not if we keep it uncovered and under nine square metres,' Zoe said. 'It's not structural, so we can just add it.'

'So, that would be three by three,' Georgia said. She pinched her chin with her fingers.

Zoe got the feeling she couldn't picture it, so she measured out a three by three metre square on the floor. 'We can make it square, like this, or pull it in and make it a little longer. And we'll make it level with the floor in here so there's no step to worry about. Plus,' Zoe said, warming to the idea herself. 'The height of the deck means you wouldn't have to put a rail on it, so the view would be unimpeded. We could just put a step down on both sides.'

Georgia glanced at the floor and wandered around it, apparently considering the size. 'That would fit a little two- or three-seater cafe table,' she said. 'Perfect for breakfast.'

'It would be,' Zoe agreed. 'Especially with the sun rising on that side.'

'Buyers will go nuts over it,' Georgia grinned. 'That's decided then.'

Zoe nodded. 'I'll measure it up and get the materials ordered.'

'Okay then. I guess I better let you get back to it,' Georgia said, turning to leave. 'Don't forget to close that window back up.'

Zoe wandered over to the window and watched Georgia drive away. After she'd disappeared, Zoe stood for a moment, looking out at the view. The rain that was forecast should green up the paddocks beyond, and that would make the French doors and small veranda worth the money. Why was it, Zoe wondered, that the thought of someone else buying and living in the cottage caused a heaviness to settle in the pit of her stomach?

Chapter 26

Ren was back to her old self by the time she and Georgia were heading out for dinner that night. They decided to go to the pub, since Ren hadn't been yet, and Monday night was two-for-one parmigiana night. Ren was a sucker for pub parmigiana, and though it wasn't Georgia's first choice of meal, she decided to get one too so they could get the discount.

'I just love country pubs,' Ren said as they sat at a table, waiting for their meals. 'Have you been here yet?'

'Last Monday night,' Georgia said. 'Zoe shouted drinks for the workers on the build after the first day.'

'Oh,' Ren said. 'So you've already had drinks with Zoe then?'

'One,' Georgia replied. 'I had one beer and then went home.'

'Right,' Ren said.

'What?' Georgia asked.

Ren leaned in and lowered her voice. 'You were complaining about her all last week, making me think she was some big, devil woman, and she turns out to be anything but. Not to mention, hot.'

Georgia rolled her eyes. 'We clashed, okay? She's stubborn and a control freak and wouldn't let me do any work.'

'Is that all it was?'

Georgia rolled her eyes. 'Stop reading stuff into nothing. I'll just be glad to finally get this place sold so I can move on with my life.'

'Well,' Ren said, pushing her chair back. 'Rick should have an idea of what it's worth soon. He's been talking to a few real estate agents about the cottage.' She stood up. 'I'm going to the loo.'

'Okay,' Georgia replied.

While Ren was gone, Georgia's attention was drawn to the beer garden where Zoe appeared to be remonstrating with someone. Georgia wondered what the poor man had done to get Zoe so hot under the collar. All of a sudden, Zoe stormed off to the bar, shaking her head.

When Ren came back, Georgia stood up. 'I'm getting another drink. Do you want one?'

'I'm good,' Ren replied.

As Georgia walked away, Ren called, 'Hey, George.'

Georgia turned.

Ren didn't say anything. She just motioned to the bar with her head and waggled her eyebrows. Georgia rolled her eyes, shook her head and walked to the bar.

'Hey,' she said, sidling up to Zoe.

Zoe turned, anger plastered all over her face. 'Hey,' she said and turned back to glare at the wall behind the bar.

'Everything okay?' Georgia asked.

'Fine,' Zoe replied bluntly.

Georgia ordered her drink and said, 'And whatever Zoe's usual is, too.'

'I didn't ask for a drink,' Zoe said, but Georgia noticed her tone had softened.

'You look like you need one. Besides, you bought me one last week. My turn tonight.'

Zoe gave Georgia a curt nod. 'Thanks.'

'No problem,' Georgia replied. She considered asking Zoe what her altercation was about, but thought better of it. Instead, she said, 'I'll see you later,' and took her drink back to her table.

When she sat down, Ren asked, 'What was that all about?'

'What?' Georgia asked.

Ren waved her hand vaguely. 'Whatever that was. Over there with Zoe.'

'Nothing,' Georgia replied. 'She bought me a drink last week, I bought her one tonight to return the favour.'

'That's it?'

'That's it,' Georgia said, sipping her wine.

Ren didn't look like she believed it, and Georgia knew there was plenty more she wanted to say, but she was stopped by the arrival of their parmigianas.

'Holy cow!' Ren said. 'Or holy chicken. Look at the size of this thing.'

Georgia stared down at the piece of chicken that was half the size of the dinner plate it was sitting on. 'We could've ordered one and shared it,' she said, lifting the corner of the chicken up to pick out a chip.

'I've been sharing my food since Caleb was born. Going away without them is the only chance I get to eat my own,' Ren said. She picked up her knife and wielded it at Georgia. 'You stay away from my food and eat your own.'

Georgia laughed. 'Fine.' As she dug in she glanced up to see Zoe was watching her, seemingly amused, from the bar. Zoe raised her beer glass to Georgia and smiled. Georgia smiled back and gave a quick nod. She glanced quickly at Ren, wondering if she'd seen the exchange, but she was too interested in her dinner to take any notice. When Georgia looked back over to the bar, Zoe was gone.

* * *

'All I'm saying,' Ren said as they walked home arm in arm. 'Is that you're here for what? Two, maybe three more weeks? Would it be so bad if you had a fling?'

Before Georgia could protest, Ren added, 'I mean, she's hot, she obviously thinks you're alright.'

'Gee, thanks,' Georgia replied. 'But I doubt that.'

Ren dug Georgia in the ribs. 'How many women have you been with since Amy died?'

'None, you know that.'

'Of course I know that. I wanted you to say it out loud and realise how pathetic that is,' Ren said.

Georgia pulled her arm away from Ren as they turned into the drive way of the motel. 'I hardly think grieving over my dead partner is pathetic.'

Ren drew in a breath and let it out with a huff. 'Look, George, I love you to bits but sometimes, you really shit me off.'

'Is that right?'

'Yes. You're your own worst enemy sometimes. What harm could a little fling with your builder do?'

'What harm? Are you serious? This is a professional relationship. Even if I wanted to, which I most certainly do not, I can't go there.'

'Can't, or won't?' Ren asked. 'Remind me again how you met Amy.'

Georgia stiffened. 'That's not fair.'

They stopped in front of Georgia's motel room door.

'Oh, that's not fair? You're saying you can't sleep with your builder because you want to keep it professional, but you met your partner of twelve years while you were helping her set up bank accounts after she left her husband?'

'Shh,' Georgia said, glancing around the car park. If anyone overheard what they were talking about, the rumour mill in such a small town would go into overdrive. 'I am not sleeping with Zoe Jennings.'

'Maybe not yet, but give it some time,' Ren replied with a grin.

'You're so bloody annoying, you know that?' Georgia said, shaking her head.

'Yeah, but you love me for it,' Ren grinned.

Georgia pulled her room key from her bag. 'You're very lucky I do,' she said. 'Are you coming up to the cottage again tomorrow morning before you leave?'

'I think I might just head off straight away,' Ren replied. 'I'm not supposed to be back until after lunch, but I want to call in to a few places on the way home.'

'I'll meet you at the cafe for breakfast then?' Georgia asked. 'About eight, is that late enough?'

'Eight's fine,' Ren replied. 'See you in the morning.' Georgia waited until Ren had closed her door before she opened her own.

As she lay in bed flicking channels later that night, she heard the tell-tale first drops of rain on the roof. Zoe had been right. Georgia picked up her phone and sent an email to Rick asking him to confirm what they were doing about the creek crossing. Then she turned the TV off and closed her eyes. Two, maybe three more weeks, and then hopefully not much longer after that, and she'd be able to pay down the mortgage on her apartment and get on with the rest of her life.

Chapter 27

Three nights of rain meant the creek at Carramar was well and truly running by the time Thursday morning rolled around. The windows still hadn't arrived back from the glazier, so they wouldn't get installed until the following week, but Zoe and Nick kicked on inside the cottage regardless.

They were installing the VJ walls in the new master bedroom by the time Georgia arrived on site mid-afternoon. Zoe sent Nick outside to grab more wall panels while she walked Georgia through the cottage and showed her their progress.

'This is looking amazing,' Georgia said. She walked over to where the kitchen was going to be. 'When is the kitchen arriving?'

'Early next week. So are the windows and the French doors. Next week is going to be a big one,' Zoe said. 'Oh! I've got something to show you.' She led

Georgia into the ensuite bathroom. Along the wall where the window was due to go in sat the refurbished claw foot bath tub. Zoe pulled the tarp off of it so Georgia could see it properly, watching for her reaction.

Georgia's eyes widened and her mouth dropped open. 'Wow,' she said. She walked over and ran her hand over the bright white tub, and then stood back and looked at it from the far wall.

'Cool, right?' Zoe said.

'Very,' Georgia agreed. 'The black on the outside makes it really stand out. I'm glad Ren talked me into putting it in here.'

'Ren?' Zoe asked. She was the one who told Georgia not to throw the tub out.

Georgia glanced up. 'And you for talking me out of dumping it.'

Georgia smiled and Zoe smiled back. She knelt down and broke open a box of tiles and took one out. 'This is the tile Celia picked out for the shower. What do you think?'

Georgia stepped closer to Zoe and ran her hands over the tile, considering it. It was a simple subway tile, larger than Zoe would normally use, but it would look amazing in the simple ensuite bathroom.

'Is this going on the floor?' Georgia asked.

'Just in the shower recess,' Zoe replied. 'We're going to stain the floors the same colour as the rest of the house and leave it timber, and Celia's suggested we switch the VJ up and run it horizontally.' Zoe wasn't convinced on that plan, but what did she know? Celia was the designer. Zoe just did as she was told. 'A few candles around the place and it will look—'

'Romantic,' Georgia said quietly.

'I was going to say sophisticated,' Zoe said. Georgia looked up and when their eyes met, Zoe almost couldn't talk. 'Romantic works though,' she managed to get out.

Georgia pulled her hand from the tile and stepped away. 'Is it usable? The tub?'

Zoe put the tile back on top of the box. 'Not yet. Celia wanted to see it in the room with the tile against it, so Nick and I set it up this morning and sent some photos through. We'll take it out this afternoon so the tilers can get started first thing Monday morning.'

'Well it looks amazing,' Georgia said. 'How are we going for time?'

'At this stage,' Zoe said. 'We're looking at a week over-run thanks to the plumbing problems we turned up yesterday, but that's not too bad considering. If we can get that sorted in the next few days, it'll be a mad rush to the finish. We're due for more rain and a storm or two over the next couple of weeks, so we'll see how we go.'

Georgia nodded. 'I wanted to talk to you about the creek crossing, too.'

'Are you getting that fixed?' Zoe asked. 'If we get more rain, you won't be able to get in here.'

'I've got a contractor coming tomorrow to have a look,' Georgia replied.

'That's not going to work,' Zoe said with a shake of her head. 'We're not working tomorrow.'

'Why not?' Georgia asked.

Zoe turned and walked out of the ensuite and back into the lounge and dining area. 'Because we're not.'

'Any particular reason?' Georgia asked, following behind.

'There doesn't have to be,' Zoe replied.

'But it's the middle of the build. You just said it was going to be a mad rush to the finish,' Georgia said. 'Shouldn't we be using the extra day to catch up some time since we're behind?'

'One day isn't going to make a difference,' Zoe said, crossing her arms.

'I understand if you can't make it, but surely someone else can be here to talk to the contractor,' Georgia said.

Zoe tried to hold in her frustration. 'Look, it was on the schedule, everyone else has made plans based on that schedule, so you're either going to have to get the contractor to come back next week, or come up yourself and meet him here.'

'You said yourself it needs to be done ASAP,' Georgia said.

'He's not going to do it tomorrow,' Zoe replied. 'And if we get the rain we're supposed to over the weekend, it won't even matter.'

'But if I don't get it done, we won't be able to get to the cottage, so we'll be further behind,' Georgia said.

'I said you won't get up here,' Zoe reminded her. 'Nick and I have four-wheel-drives, so we'll be fine.'

Georgia crossed her arms and glared at Zoe. 'You don't want me here.'

'That's not what I said,' Zoe replied, rolling her eyes.

'You may as well have,' Georgia replied.

Zoe sighed heavily. 'Look, I can't make it up here because I've got other plans. I can get Nick to meet you here if you want someone else to talk to him, but honestly, he'll know what you want when he sees it.'

'Whatever,' Georgia replied. 'Is that it, then?'

'I guess so,' Zoe said.

They stood and eye-balled each other for a moment before Zoe finally turned away. 'I have to get back to these walls.'

'Is there anything I can do while I'm here?' Georgia asked.

'You can undercoat the trims,' Zoe replied. 'That will buy us some of that precious time you're so worried about. The timber's stacked in the shed and I presume you know where everything else is.'

'Fine,' Georgia huffed and walked back outside.

Zoe let out a breath and looked around the cottage. She'd have to go get more wall panels herself, since Nick seemed to be taking his time.

Chapter 28

Georgia hated to admit it, but Zoe had been right about the contractor. When she met him at the cottage the next morning, he told Georgia exactly what he was going to do to fix the creek crossing, and she didn't understand any of it. As long as he made it so cars could get in and out when the creek was running, that was good enough for her.

She told him to email a quote through to Rick, but the fact that he could have a crew out and started by next Tuesday morning meant he'd get the job. It needed to be done, and Georgia couldn't see a need to go and chase down other quotes in the hope of finding someone cheaper. She didn't want to add any more time to the build than was necessary.

After the contractor left, Georgia decided to head to the cottage and finish undercoating the trims. She may as well get that finished while she was out there.

As she wound her way up the driveway, she noticed the dark clouds forming in the sky to the west. Zoe had warned her a couple of times of the storms, but she figured she had enough time to get the trims finished before she headed back to the motel. Judging by the progress on the cottage, there was probably nothing else she'd be able to do herself to help out, but getting the trims finished would be one job done.

The way Zoe had been hot and cold over the last few days, Georgia wasn't sure she wanted to be on site any more than she had to be. Maybe she'd wait around until the creek crossing was started and then she'd head back home to the city until the cottage was finished. With all the roadworks going on again, she wouldn't get her car up, and besides, it would be good to get back to her apartment and stop living out of a suitcase.

After an hour or so of painting, the rumble of thunder caught Georgia by surprise. It was much closer than she'd imagined. She'd heard a few rumbles earlier but dismissed them. She put her paint brush down into the pot and walked outside. Having a light on in the shed where she was painting had given her a false sense of how dark it had gotten outside.

She walked out to the front yard and looked across to the west, where the storm was coming from. From her vantage point on top of the hill, she could see the rain streaming down across the valley. If she hurried, she could get the last couple of trims finished and then head back into town.

* * *

Georgia was cleaning out her paint brush when the crack of lightning made her jump. She dropped the brush in a pot of water, figuring it would be fine until Monday morning, picked up her things and hurried to her car. As she climbed in to the driver's seat, the first drops of rain started falling, and by the time she'd driven a few hundred metres down the driveway, the sky had opened up.

Rain poured down as Georgia slowed the car to a crawl, navigating the dirt driveway as best she could as it became more and more slippery. She hoped the creek was still low enough for her to cross to get out onto the road. Once she was on bitumen, she'd be fine.

As she came around a corner, her tyres slid on loose gravel and mud and in her attempt to pull the car back across to the centre, Georgia only succeeded in sliding it straight into the ditch. She cursed and threw the car into reverse. She put her foot down, but the car didn't move.

She tried again, and the tyres got some purchase but just when she thought she was free, they slid again, sending her back into the ditch. She was stuck.

She pulled out her phone to make a phone call, but she had no signal. 'Damn it!' She'd just have to sit in her car and wait out the storm until she could walk back to the cottage and find a signal.

It took almost an hour for the storm to clear and not wanting to take any chances, Georgia gave it a good ten minutes to make sure it had stopped raining before she got out of the car. She grabbed her bag, locked up her car and started the long walk back up the hill, trying not to slip over on the muddy driveway.

Just as she made it to the last bend, the skies opened up again.

'Just bloody perfect,' Georgia mumbled, as she broke out into a jog.

Relief flooded through her when she spotted the cottage through the gloom, but it was short-lived as her foot stuck in a puddle of thick mud, sending her tumbling to the ground. She lay there for a moment, almost too shocked to do anything.

She pushed herself up off the ground and when she finally trudged into the shed, she was soaking wet, covered in mud, and freezing cold. She wiped her hands on a rag and pulled her phone from her bag, making sure it was still dry and checking for a signal. She had one bar. Maybe enough for a phone call if she stood still enough. Against her better judgement, she dialled Zoe's number first but got voice mail. She left a voice message but the signal dropped out before she could finish it. She called Jennings Construction's office number, but it rang out too.

In desperation, she called Ren, but it dropped out when Ren picked up. She wanted to throw her phone across the room, but took a deep breath to calm herself. Her phone dinged. It was a message from Ren.

Did you butt dial me?

She could get messages at least, which meant she could send them. She tried to think of a way to tell Ren what had happened without worrying her. She settled on *Ph signal bad Stuck at cottage Can Rick call Jack Jennings to get someone to come get me?*

Ren text back almost immediately. *Why are you stuck at the cottage? What's happened?*

Georgia replied *I'm fine Just need a lift that's all.* She hoped Ren wouldn't ask any more questions.

Ren sent back *Rick calling Jack now What's going on?*

Georgia didn't want to get into it right now, so she replied *Will call you later*

Ren text back *You better Jack sending someone to come get you.*

Georgia smiled in spite of herself and her situation and text Ren back. *Thanks xx*

She unfolded a camp chair and looked around for something dry she could wrap herself in. The chill was starting to set in, and rain was falling steadily outside. She spied the painting drop sheet she'd been using earlier. She flicked it out and then pulled it around herself and sat on the camp chair. The only thing she could do now was to wait for whoever Jack had organised to come and get her.

Chapter 29

Zoe had just pulled her swag from the back of her ute when Jack called. 'What's up?'

'Have you left yet?' Jack asked.

'Just about to. I decided to wait for that last storm to go through. Why?'

'I just had a call from Rick Wheeler—'

'Are you bloody kidding me?' Zoe set her jaw and shook her head. 'What the hell have I done now?'

'Nothing,' Jack said. 'Something's happened with Georgia Ballantyne.'

A chill crept up Zoe's neck. 'What's she done?'

'She's stuck up at the cottage apparently. Needs someone to go and get her,' Jack replied.

Zoe let out a breath, whatever worry she'd been feeling turning to anger. 'I bloody warned her about that creek. I bet she's stuck in her car sitting on the other side of it.'

'I don't know,' Jack said. 'Rick just said they got a text from Georgia asking for them to send someone up to the cottage.'

'Why the hell did she call them for?' Zoe asked.

'I don't know,' Jack replied. 'But she did, and then he called me.'

'Why are you telling me?'

'Because you're going to have to go and get her,' Jack said.

'I am bloody not,' Zoe said. 'You know tonight's my night away.'

'I know that, Zo. I called Nick first but he's practising for his Mister Elizabeth Creek thing, so it has to be you.'

Zoe closed her eyes and let out a breath. 'Fine. I'll go and get her but she's not allowed back on site 'til the end of the build.'

'Zo,' Jack started.

'No, Jack. She's causing me too much grief. There's nothing else she can do up there anyway, except get in the way. I'll bring her back to the motel and she can bloody well stay there.'

'We'll talk about it tomorrow,' Jack said. 'Let me know when she's safe so I can let Rick know.'

'Sure,' Zoe said and hung up. She banged her head against the steering wheel. 'Bloody Georgia Ballantyne.'

She started her car and drove toward Carramar cottage, the opposite direction to which she should have been heading.

* * *

By the time Zoe reached the creek crossing at Carramar, it was getting dark. She pulled her ute up at the edge of the creek, took a torch from her seat and got out. She shone the torch up and down the creek and checked its depth. It wasn't running overly fast, but with more rain coming later on and with this part of the creek being at the bottom of the hill, the water was bound to get higher. It was crossable for the moment, but Zoe guessed it wouldn't be for much longer.

She turned off the torch, tossed it in the cab and climbed back in. She drove slowly across the creek and out the other side, and was surprised that she didn't see Georgia's car anywhere.

She drove up the rise and around the first corner and spotted Georgia's car sitting sideways in the ditch. 'Ah, shit.'

Zoe pulled up, leaving the ute running and jumped out, checking Georgia's car. She wasn't inside it, and there wasn't much damage, but the front wheels were stuck fast in the mud. That car wasn't going anywhere until tomorrow. Zoe climbed back into her ute and drove on, hoping Georgia had made it back to the cottage.

She drove up past the cottage, scanning for any sign of Georgia. All of the anger she had at missing her trip melted away when she pulled up in front of the shed and saw Georgia soaking wet and huddled on a chair, wrapped in a drop sheet. If she didn't know any better, she'd have thought she'd felt a tinge of affection, but she pushed the thought down as she stepped down from the ute. Georgia jumped up when she saw the car, shielding her face from the car lights.

Zoe turned the engine and lights off and got out. 'What the bloody hell happened?'

'You?' Georgia replied.

'Yes, me. Who else did you think would be coming?'

Georgia threw off the drop sheet, grabbed her bag and headed for the ute. She was caked in mud. Had she tried to pull herself out of the ditch?

'Where are you going?' Zoe asked.

'Back to the motel, I assume. And a nice hot shower.'

Zoe shook her head. 'We're not going anywhere just yet. The creek's up and it's getting higher. We're going to have to wait it out.'

Georgia looked stricken and Zoe noticed she was shivering.

'You're cold,' Zoe said.

'I'm fine,' Georgia replied hugging her arms around herself and trudging back to the shed. She picked up the drop sheet, pulled it around her shoulders and dropped back into the chair. Zoe pulled her bag out of the tray of the ute. She pulled out a blanket and gave it to Georgia. 'Here. This'll keep you warmer.'

At first, Georgia didn't take it. 'I'll get mud on it,' she mumbled.

'Just take the bloody thing,' Zoe ordered. 'You need to get warm.'

Georgia did as she was told, passing the drop sheet to Zoe and swapping it for the blanket.

Zoe pulled out her phone and called Jack. 'Georgia's fine,' she said when he answered. 'Can you do me a favour and check the rain radar?'

'Looks like there's some more rain coming,' Jack replied.

'Okay, thanks. The creek's up here, so I think we'll stay up here overnight.'

'What about your night away?' Jack asked.

'Well, technically I'm still away,' Zoe replied. She glanced over to where Georgia was huddled into the blanket, trying to get warm. 'Just not where I was supposed to be.'

'Okay, well, I guess I'll see you in the morning,' Jack said.

'I guess so,' Zoe replied. She hung up and walked back over to the shed.

'How can you make phone calls and I can't?' Georgia asked.

'I've got a range extender,' Zoe replied. She started pulling her camping gear and swag from the back of her ute.

'What are you doing?' Georgia asked.

'We're stuck here tonight,' Zoe said. 'And since I was going out tonight anyway, I might as well make use of my gear.'

She unpacked her food onto the table and pulled out her bottle of scotch. She held it for moment, considering whether to just put it back away again. She only drank this scotch once a year. She let out a breath. If not now, she'd have to wait another year. She unscrewed the top, took a drink and closed her eyes as she swallowed. And then she turned and handed the bottle to Georgia.

'Here. This will warm you up a bit while I get everything sorted.'

Georgia took the bottle and took a drink, coughing it down.

'Bloody hell, what is this stuff?' Georgia asked, pulling a face.

'Dad's favourite,' Zoe replied. 'Puts fire in your belly, he used to say.'

Georgia nodded and then took another drink. 'He wasn't wrong.'

Zoe took the bottle back, had another drink and then capped it. Then she unpacked the urn from the lock box, filled it with water and plugged it in.

'I could do with a coffee,' Georgia said, rubbing her hands on her arms.

'It's not for coffee,' Zoe replied.

'What's it for?'

Zoe dug around in her rucksack and pulled out a small bag. 'You need to get out of your wet clothes, so I'm making you a bath.'

'Um, I don't mean to sound dumb, but how exactly?' Georgia asked.

Zoe nodded to the cast iron tub in the corner, covered in a tarp. 'In that,' she said. 'I'll be back in a minute.' She took the keys from the ute, threw her swag over her shoulder and headed to the cottage.

Chapter 30

It took four urn refills to get enough hot water in the tub for a hot bath, and although this was so far from what Georgia was wanting right now, it was her only choice. Zoe had plugged up the drainage hole with rags, and had dug a ditch of sorts for the water to run off as it seeped out.

'I'm not sure how long it'll hold out for,' Zoe said, hands on hips. 'So you might want to be quick.'

Georgia stood beside the tub, her arms crossed, glaring at Zoe. She raised her eyebrows and cocked her head. 'Can I get some privacy at least?'

Zoe looked away. 'Oh, right. Sorry. I'll just…' She pointed back over her shoulder. 'Go set up camp inside the cottage.' She turned and grabbed her rucksack and walked out of the shed.

Georgia waited until Zoe had disappeared into the cottage before she hurriedly stripped off and dipped a toe into the water. It was steaming hot but the cold air had cooled it at least a little, and Zoe had left an upturned bucket beside it with a cake of soap. How Zoe managed to have a cake of soap with her was something Georgia would ask later. But for now, she was concentrating on getting warm and clean.

She eased herself down into the tub, the cold of the cast iron on her skin contrasting with the heat of the water. When she finally got settled, she closed her eyes and breathed in the warm steam. Under different circumstances, she'd be enjoying this immensely. She lay back and relaxed as she felt the warmth creeping back into her body. She knew she was supposed to be scrubbing the mud off, but she hadn't had a bath in such a long time, she figured she may as well enjoy it, at least for the moment.

It didn't take long before Georgia realised that the water level had started dropping more rapidly, so she decided it was time she should actually get herself clean. She took the soap from the upturned bucket and began to lather herself, the water turning a murky brown as she scrubbed off the mud and dirt. There was a noise at the door, and Georgia scrunched down into the tub and turned her head.

Zoe was standing in the doorway, her head down, one hand shielding her eyes, the other holding a towel and clothes. 'Sorry. This was down the bottom of my bag. Thought you might need it.'

'Thanks,' Georgia replied.

'I'll just, ah…' Zoe crept in tentatively, and took a camp chair and pushed it close to the tub with her foot. She hung the towel over the back of the chair and put the clothes on the seat. 'I brought you some clean clothes too. They're mine, obviously, so they might not fit but at least they'll be dry.'

Georgia was surprised to find herself amused at Zoe's obvious attempts to not accidentally see her naked. Especially after she'd been checking out her butt only a week ago. 'Thanks.'

Zoe nodded and turned and walked away. She stopped in the doorway. 'When you're ready, come up to the house. We'll have something to eat.'

'Okay,' Georgia replied and watched as Zoe hurried away back to the cottage. She finished washing herself and unblocked the drain, the water creating a river of mud as it leaked across the floor of the shed and ran off under the wall. She towelled herself dry in the tub so she didn't get dirt on her feet, and then put on the jeans, t-shirt and jumper Zoe had left her. They were a little big for Georgia, especially the jeans, which were looser fitting than she'd wear herself, but they were dry and comforting. She shoved her feet into her boots and picked her way carefully across the yard to the cottage. Lightning lit up the sky in the distance, a sign more rain was coming, and having taken off her muddy boots and left them just inside the door, Georgia hurried inside the cottage.

Muted light illuminated the back of the house and the smell of something rich and meaty drifted from inside. Georgia's mouth watered and her stomach grumbled. How long had it been since she'd eaten? She couldn't remember.

She walked through the new extension to find the source of the light and smell and found Zoe hunched over a gas burner in one of the bedrooms in the old part of the cottage. Zoe's swag was rolled out on the floor against one wall, and a sleeping bag was laid out on the floor across from it.

'That smells amazing,' Georgia said, standing in the doorway, unsure where she should sit.

Zoe looked up and, Georgia noticed, looked her up and down before looking back at the pot she was stirring. 'My sister-in-law's stew,' Zoe said. 'How was the bath?'

'Good,' Georgia replied. 'I feel much better. Thanks.'

Zoe nodded. 'You can have the swag. It'll be more comfortable than the sleeping bag.'

Georgia stepped across the room and sat on the swag, crossing her legs underneath her. She wasn't sure why Zoe was being so nice to her, but she wasn't about to question it with the prospect of a warm bowl of stew on offer. 'Thanks for the clothes.'

'You needed some dry ones,' Zoe replied not looking up. 'They look like they fit okay.'

'They do, surprisingly well,' Georgia said.

Zoe turned off the gas cooker and spooned stew onto a plate and handed it to Georgia. She ate her own meal straight from the pot. Georgia didn't know whether it was because she was hungry or not, but the stew was amazingly good.

'Oh my God,' she said.

Zoe smiled. 'Good, right?'

'Uh-huh,' Georgia agreed as she savoured another spoonful of the delicious beef and vegetables.

They ate in silence for a while until Georgia said, 'You were going camping tonight?'

Zoe nodded, but didn't say anything.

'I'm sorry I messed up your plans.'

Zoe shrugged. 'I'm still camping, technically. Just not where I thought I'd be.'

'Probably drier,' Georgia said.

'Probably,' Zoe replied.

Georgia scraped her plate clean of gravy and considered wiping it clean with her finger, but decided against it. She placed her plate on the floor and shuffled back on the swag so she could lean against the wall.

Zoe put the pot on the floor and pulled out the bottle of scotch. She uncapped it and took a drink before handing it to Georgia.

'Is there some special reason you were going camping tonight? Or it's just something you do?' Georgia asked, taking the scotch and having a drink.

Zoe took the scotch back, had another drink and said, 'It's the anniversary of my parents' deaths.'

Georgia's heart dropped into her stomach. 'Oh, God, I'm so sorry.'

'It's okay,' Zoe said. 'It was a long time ago.'

'Yes, but I've totally messed up your night,' Georgia said.

'Forget it,' Zoe said. She picked up the pot, plate and cutlery and stood up. 'I'm going to clean these up, and then we should get some sleep.'

Georgia wondered whether there was more to the story than Zoe was letting on. She didn't do anything to commemorate Amy's death. In fact, apart from the funeral, Georgia tried her best to ignore anything to do with the date Amy died.

Georgia pulled back the cover of the swag and lay on the mattress underneath. It was more comfortable than it looked. She pulled the cover over herself and turned onto her side.

Zoe was only gone for a few minutes before she was back in the room packing up the plates and other dishes into a small esky. 'Okay if I turn this off now?' she asked, indicating the LED lamp.

Georgia nodded.

Zoe turned off the lamp, turning the room pitch black until Georgia's eyes adjusted to the gloom. She heard the sleeping bag rustle across from her as Zoe got settled.

The thunder rolled closer outside and a crack of lightning lit up the sky, illuminating the room. She locked eyes with Zoe, who was lying on her side, apparently watching Georgia. When the next round of lightning lit up the room, Zoe had turned onto her back. Georgia had a feeling there was more to Zoe Jennings than she let on.

'Goodnight,' Georgia said into the dark.

There was a moment when Georgia thought Zoe might have already been asleep, until Zoe replied, 'Night.'

Chapter 31

Zoe was up with the sun the next morning and quietly snuck outside to the shed, where she boiled some water for coffee and made a start on breakfast. There really wasn't enough for two people, but she'd grab something more to eat at home before she headed to the workshop. She needed to finish sanding and painting the doors for the cottage if she was going to get this build finished on time.

She'd lay awake for hours last night, listening to the storm roll in and then over them, and then to Georgia sleeping across the room. Zoe wondered if Georgia knew she snored. Not like a freight train, like Zoe's father used to, but more like loud, deep breaths with the occasional snort. Zoe found herself smiling at the memory. She had to admit that it was sort of cute.

'Morning,' Georgia said, bringing Zoe out of her thoughts. She looked up from the pan. Georgia was leaning on the door frame, her eyes still sleepy and her hair pushed up on one side. The sight of her like that, just barely awake, made Zoe's insides turn to mush. She swallowed hard and turned her attention back to cooking breakfast.

'There's not much,' Zoe said. 'I only brought enough for me, obviously, but there's enough to take the edge off until we get into town.'

'That's okay,' Georgia replied. 'I'm still full from that stew last night.' She pushed away from the door frame and wandered into the shed. 'Any chance I can get coffee?'

Zoe pointed to the table. 'There's some hot water in the urn. I figured you might want some warm water to wash up this morning, so I heated it up again. Everything else is in the lock boxes. Help yourself.'

Georgia smiled and proceeded to make two coffees and handed one to Zoe. She accepted it gratefully and took a sip. 'Perfect.'

'Well, I've been making them for you for the last two weeks, I should know how you like it,' Georgia said. She smiled over the top of her mug.

Zoe smiled back and then looked away, concentrating on dividing the eggs and bacon onto two plates, and handed one to Georgia. As they ate, Zoe said, 'We'll see if we can pull your car out on our way back into town. From what I saw last night, it just slid into the ditch.'

'I don't think I'll be bringing it back up here,' Georgia said. 'Not if we're going to be getting more rain.'

'It's supposed to clear by the end of the week so you should be okay next week, but you'll have to come up here with me or Nick in the mean time,' Zoe said. 'And as for the creek, we'll have to wait and see if it's still up or not when we get there. The second storm was more bluster than anything else, so we might get lucky.'

Georgia nodded. She finished her breakfast and then said, 'I'm sorry I messed up your plans last night.'

Zoe looked up from her plate. 'It's okay.'

Georgia stood up, put her plate onto the table and walked over to the bath tub. 'Ugh, I guess I should clean that before it goes back in the house.'

'What happened, to get you caked in mud like that last night?' Zoe asked. 'Did you try and dig yourself out?'

Georgia bit her bottom lip and took a sip of her coffee. 'I tripped over,' she said.

'Where?'

'Just out there.' Georgia pointed outside the shed. 'It was raining so I started running once I saw the cottage and just as I got to the corner, my foot hit a puddle. I slipped and went face first into the mud.'

Zoe laughed out loud. 'Sorry, it's not funny, really. You didn't hurt anything, did you?'

'Apart from my pride?' Georgia replied.

Zoe's phone buzzed in her pocket. It was a message from Jack. *Just wanted to see how you were.*

Zoe sent him a quick text back. *All good Heading back to town soon Catch up later.*

Jack sent back a thumbs up and Zoe said to Georgia, 'We should get going. I've got a class today, and I'm guessing you want to have a long hot shower?'

Georgia nodded. 'I'm looking forward to it.'

Zoe stood up. 'We should clean this stuff up so we can go rescue your car.'

* * *

The creek at the bottom of the driveway was still underwater, so once they pulled Georgia's car out of the ditch, they left it at the cottage and Zoe drove them both back into town. When they pulled up at the motel, Georgia said, 'Look, I know I didn't sound like it last night, but I'm really grateful you came out to the cottage to get me.'

'Far as I can tell, neither of us were happy with the positions we were in last night, so…' Zoe shrugged.

'Yeah, well, things didn't end up too badly,' Georgia said. 'Did they?'

Zoe shook her head. 'No, they didn't.'

Georgia looked like she wanted to say something else, but instead she said, 'Well, I guess I'll see you on Monday.'

Zoe nodded and as Georgia turned to walk away, she said, 'You should come to the workshop.' She didn't know why she said it, but for some reason, she wanted to show Georgia the place she felt most at home. And she had those doors to show her for the cottage.

'The workshop? What for?' Georgia asked.

Zoe ran her hand over the back of her head. 'I've got some doors there I think might be good for the cottage. If you want to take a look, and I take a carpentry class. With kids. We're making boxes for the show next weekend.'

'A carpentry class? Are you trying to tell me I need practice?' Georgia's mischievous smile sent a ripple through Zoe's body.

Zoe grinned. 'Well, if you're going to be filling in for Nick next week, then you're going to have to learn the basics.'

'Where's Nick going?' Georgia asked.

'He's practising dancing and strutting for the Mister Elizabeth Creek competition all week. It's like a showgirl competition but for the blokes,' Zoe explained.

'Right,' Georgia replied. 'I guess I might see you later, then.'

'Around one,' Zoe said. As she pulled away, she glanced into her review mirror to see Georgia still standing on the footpath. Zoe stuck her arm out the window and waved, and Georgia waved back and turned and walked up the motel driveway.

As Zoe drove home, she couldn't shake the feeling that something had shifted between them. Something that had made her panic as soon as she'd seen

Georgia's car in the ditch, thinking she'd been hurt. Something that made her heart beat a little faster when she'd lay awake last night, close enough to Georgia to hear her breathing in her sleep.

What surprised her, though, was that her instinct to tamp down on her feelings had seemed to have disappeared. She wasn't sure that was a good thing or not yet, but she was willing to find out.

Chapter 32

After a long hot shower, and catching up on some sleep, Georgia checked in with Ren to let her know she was still alive. Ren wanted 'all the goss' about Zoe and hadn't believed it when Georgia insisted there was none.

'The two of you alone in a storm and nothing happened? I don't believe it,' Ren had said.

'You read way too many romance novels,' Georgia had replied.

'Can't say I'm not disappointed,' Ren had answered. 'But there's still time.'

Georgia had hung up soon after, but as she walked down to the cafe for lunch, the thought did niggle at her brain about the subtle shift she'd felt between her and Zoe. Had Zoe felt it too over the last few days?

The cafe wasn't busy when Georgia arrived, and she ordered a salad at the counter and turned to find a table by the window. She was about to sit down when someone called her name. She turned to see Jack at a table in the back with a woman and two kids who Georgia assumed were his family. The boy looked vaguely familiar and it took a moment to realise he was the one at Leroy's a couple of weeks ago. He was concentrating on a bowl of chips, his face covered in tomato sauce. The little girl, who Georgia guessed was his sister, jiggled her feet under the table as she drank from a milkshake.

Jack introduced Georgia to his wife, Molly and to Ryan and Josie and said, 'Zoe said you got out alright this morning.'

Georgia nodded. 'The creek was still up so we left my car there until it goes down.'

'It goes down as quick as it comes up,' Jack said. 'So shouldn't be more than a day or two.'

'That's what Zoe said,' Georgia replied.

'Sorry I had to send her last night,' Jack said. 'I know you two haven't been getting on well. She can be a bit over the top if you don't know her.'

'She was fine,' Georgia assured him. 'I'm just sorry I interrupted her camping trip.' She was unsure if she should mention that she knew the reason for it, so she erred on the side of caution. 'We had a pretty good night, actually.'

'Really?' Molly asked. Georgia found it intriguing that she sounded surprised by that information.

'Oh, and by the way, that stew of yours was amazing,' Georgia said. 'I can't remember the last time I ate a stew like that.'

'Zoe shared her food?' Molly asked, raising an eyebrow.

Georgia nodded. 'And her scotch, which I have to say, although it burned my insides out, did warm me up.'

Molly and Jack glanced at each other and Georgia got the feeling she was being left out of an in joke.

'I'm not going to grow an extra head or something, am I?' Georgia joked.

'It was Dad's favourite, that scotch,' Jack said. 'I'm not sure Zoe told you, but yesterday was the anniversary of our parents' deaths.'

'She mentioned that,' Georgia said. 'So she goes camping and drinks bad scotch to commemorate it?'

'Something like that,' Jack said. 'I can't believe there's still some left, though. The distillery that made it went out of business years ago. Robbo's got the last carton and Zoe's the only one who buys it.'

'I don't know what she's going to do when it runs out,' Molly said.

'She might have to finally deal with it like an adult,' Jack huffed.

Molly put her hand on Jack's shoulder. 'I think she's dealing with it the way she needs to, Love.' She smiled at Georgia. 'She's not as tough as she makes out, you know.'

Georgia had certainly seen some of that softer side last night, and it intrigued her that someone as forthright and blunt as Zoe had a soft centre.

A waitress interrupted their conversation, bringing Georgia her lunch.

'We should let you go,' Molly said. 'We're almost ready to head off anyway. Ryan wants to call in to Zoe's workshop to work on his box for the show.'

'Oh, I'm heading down there after lunch,' Georgia said. She smiled at Ryan. 'I might see you there.'

Ryan replied by shoving a chip into his mouth.

'She hasn't roped you into a class, has she?' Jack joked.

Georgia shook her head. 'She said she's got some doors that might suit the cottage, so I was going to have a look.'

'Right,' Jack said. 'We might see you down there then.'

'You might,' Georgia replied. 'It was really great meeting you all.'

'You too,' Molly replied.

Georgia left Jack and his family to finish their lunch and sat at a table by the window.

As she ate her lunch, she thought about what Jack and Molly had said about Zoe not dealing with her parents' deaths. And even though Zoe hadn't made a fuss about it last night, Georgia thought that there was maybe more to it than she'd said.

Georgia could certainly relate to Zoe not dealing with the death of her parents. Even though Amy's cancer had meant that her death wasn't unexpected in the end, Georgia had found it hard to deal with initially. It wasn't just not having Amy when she needed her and reached for her. It was all those lost moments and experiences they'd never get to have together that tore at Georgia, at least in the beginning.

Which was the reason the cottage had to go. It was the last thing tying Georgia to Amy, and she knew that no matter what memories that cottage would have held for them both, they'd never get to experience them now. With the cottage sold, Georgia might finally be able to move on with her life after Amy. She wondered what it would take for Zoe to move on.

Chapter 33

Zoe was helping Ryan sand his box when her phone buzzed in her pocket. She nestled it between her ear and shoulder. 'Zoe Jennings.'

'It's Georgia. Ballantyne.'

'Oh, hey. Hang on a sec.' Zoe waved at Nick to come and take over and headed for the door. 'Everything okay?'

'I'm standing outside your workshop,' Georgia said. 'But there's no-one here.'

Zoe glanced around but couldn't see anyone, and then it hit her. 'Oh, you're at the work shed?'

'Isn't that where you said?' Georgia asked.

'Sorry,' Zoe replied. 'I should've been more specific. I use a workshop just up the road for my classes. I can come and get you if you like?'

'How far is it?' Georgia asked.

'A couple of blocks from where you are,' Zoe replied. Someone tugged at her shirt and she looked down to see Ryan holding out a coloured block, waiting for her approval. She gave him a thumbs up and he grinned and raced back inside.

'I can walk down if it's not far. Just tell me where,' Georgia said.

Zoe shifted the phone to her other ear and peered back in to the workshop to check on Nick. 'Keep walking past the work shed and take the first right into Sussex.'

'Okay,' Georgia replied, and from the slight puff in her voice, Zoe guessed she'd started walking as she gave instructions.

'You'll walk past a little church on the right and then cross over the next road and I'm half-way along in an old timber shed. You'll probably hear us before you see us.'

'Church on the right, cross the road, timber shed,' Georgia replied. 'Got it. I'll see you soon.'

Zoe hung up and went back inside the shed to let Nick know she was ducking out for a minute or two. Then she walked back out to the footpath and shielded her eyes from the sun as she waited for Georgia to arrive. She spotted her as she crossed the street and waved. When Georgia waved back, a warmth settled in her chest.

'Hey,' Georgia said as she strode up the driveway.

'Sorry, I should have made sure you knew which shed I was talking about. I forget sometimes,' Zoe apologised.

Georgia shook her head. 'That's okay. I'm here now.'

They stood there smiling at each other for a moment until Zoe remembered why she was there. 'So, I'll show you those doors. If you like them we can get started on prepping them.' She turned and led Georgia inside the workshop, where the kids were in full swing, hammering and sanding.

Georgia stuck around for the rest of the afternoon, offering to get started on stripping the paint from the doors and sanding them while Zoe finished up with her class. Zoe wasn't going to argue. The more work that got done on the doors before they were installed, the easier they'd be to finish on site.

After Nick and the kids had left, Zoe wandered over to check on Georgia's progress. She'd almost finished with one door, which was impressive. Georgia looked up and pulled her dust mask down onto her chin.

'What do you think, boss?' she joked.

Zoe ran her hands along the timber and nodded. 'Not bad for an apprentice.'

'Oh, is that what I am now?' Georgia asked, eyebrow raised.

'Everyone's got to start somewhere,' Zoe replied. They smiled at each other for a bit and then Zoe said, 'Want to take a break?'

'Sure,' Georgia said. She pulled the dust mask over her head and placed it on the door with her gloves and safety glasses.

Zoe led them to the back of the shed where her bar fridge was kept and pulled out a couple of beers. She opened the top of one and handed it to Georgia and then opened hers and took a long drink. She wandered over to the bench and pulled herself up to sit on it. Georgia did the same.

'Cheers,' Georgia said.

They clinked bottles and as she took a drink, Zoe watched as Georgia glanced around the workshop.

'It's a lot neater than I thought it would be,' Georgia said.

'That's just because I've been moving stuff out,' Zoe replied. 'Usually that rack over there is full of tools, and there's a big pile of old timber stacked over there by the door.'

'You're moving out?' Georgia asked.

'Not by choice,' Zoe replied, taking a long drink of her beer.

'Oh?'

Zoe sucked in a breath and let it out. 'Long story short, I was going to buy the place, but it was sold from under me.'

'Oh, I'm sorry to hear that,' Georgia said. 'Have you got anywhere else to go?'

'We aren't exactly swimming in empty old workshops here,' Zoe replied. 'I'm storing stuff at work until I find somewhere but until then?' She shrugged.

'How long have you got left in here?' Georgia asked.

'A couple more weeks. Today was my last class with the kids.' Zoe shook her head. 'I just had so many plans for this place, you know?'

'Yeah,' Georgia replied. 'I do.'

Zoe glanced at Georgia. She was smiling one of those smiles where your mouth said you were happy but your eyes didn't agree. She wondered what could make Georgia feel like that, and not wanting to upset her by asking, Zoe cleared her throat and jumped down off the bench. 'So, should we finish all of these doors? Or do you want to get back to your motel?'

Georgia pushed herself off the bench. 'I'm happy to keep going if you are.'

'We should have enough beer in the fridge to see us through,' Zoe said with a nod.

'Sold,' Georgia grinned.

'Right, then,' Zoe nodded. 'We're going to need some music.' Zoe walked over to the wall near the door, turned on the old radio and turned it up. Then she grabbed her dust mask and a door and placed it on the bench across from Georgia and got started on stripping away the paint.

Every now and then, she glanced up to see Georgia working away on her door. Apart from her classes and occasionally Nick and Jack, she didn't often share the workspace with anyone else. Not like this anyway. For the first time in a long time, she felt content.

* * *

Hours later, as Zoe was wiping down the last door, Molly walked into the workshop. Zoe didn't hear her thanks to the radio, and she jumped when Molly tapped her on the shoulder to grab her attention. She checked her watch and threw back her head. 'I'm so sorry, Mol. I've done it again.'

Molly leaned in and raised her voice over the radio. 'I thought I'd find you wallowing over here, but I can see I was totally wrong about that.' She nodded over to Georgia, who was on the far end of the bench, wiping down her doors. She obviously hadn't heard Molly come in either.

'I can see why you lost track of time,' Molly said with a smile.

'We were just getting some work done,' Zoe replied, turning down the radio.

'Whatever you say,' Molly said, but Zoe got the impression she didn't believe her. She handed Zoe a container. 'Spaghetti. I brought enough for lunch tomorrow, or you know, it would be enough for two if that's what you wanted.'

'Hey, Molly!' Georgia called from the other end of the workshop. She dropped her rag into her bucket of water and walked down and stood beside Zoe.

'I brought some dinner,' she said.

'Oh?' Georgia said, looking at Zoe, mildly confused.

'If Zoe doesn't make dinner, this is usually where I can find her,' Molly explained. 'It's her happy place.'

Zoe rolled her eyes. Molly made her sound like a child needing to find a place to hide whenever she felt bad. Which if she thought about it, wasn't actually too far from the truth, but she wasn't about to admit that in front of Georgia.

'There's enough there for two,' Molly said, not even trying to be subtle.

'Only one set of cutlery,' Zoe replied without thinking and then realised how that must have sounded.

'Oh, that's okay. I should probably get going anyway,' Georgia said.

'I can drop you off,' Zoe said. 'Save you walking.' She hoped Georgia hadn't taken the cutlery comment as an insult, and the least she could do was drop her home.

'Are you sure?' Georgia asked.

'Of course,' Zoe smiled.

'I should get home too,' Molly said. 'If you haven't got any plans tomorrow, Georgia, you're welcome out to our place for lunch.'

'I wouldn't want to intrude,' Georgia replied.

'You wouldn't be,' Molly said with a wave of her hand. 'Besides, I'm trying out recipes for my scones to enter into the show next weekend. I could use an unbiased opinion.'

Zoe rolled her eyes. 'I'm sure Georgia has more important things to do.'

Georgia shook her head. 'Not really. Besides, I do love a good scone.'

'Is that right?' Molly asked. 'That's settled then. I'll see you tomorrow.'

Zoe and Georgia walked Molly out, and waved her off as she drove down the road.

'I guess I should shut up shop and get you home,' Zoe said.

'I guess so,' Georgia replied.

Zoe handed Georgia the container of spaghetti and headed back inside the workshop to lock up.

Chapter 34

As they pulled up in front of the motel, Zoe asked, 'Did you have any plans for dinner?'

'Not really,' Georgia replied. To be honest, she hadn't really thought about it because until Molly had arrived at the workshop, Georgia had totally lost track of the time. But if Zoe was asking her out for dinner, she certainly wouldn't say no. They'd had a great night at the workshop, at least Georgia thought so, and she wouldn't mind spending some time with Zoe outside of work.

She had a feeling she'd seen Zoe in her element at her workshop, teaching the kids in her class that afternoon and then showing her how to prep the doors. She seemed to be a natural at teaching, which is why Nick probably liked working for her so much.

'I'm happy to share my spaghetti,' Zoe offered. 'If you want to. I mean, Molly always gives me way too much anyway.'

'Only if you're happy to,' Georgia said, remembering Molly's surprise that morning about Zoe sharing her food last night.

'Of course,' Zoe replied. 'But only if you've got some cutlery. Otherwise one of us will be eating with our hands.'

'I think I can find some,' Georgia replied with a smile.

When they got to Georgia's room, she said, 'Sorry about the mess. I wasn't expecting visitors.'

'It's okay,' Zoe said as she stepped inside. 'You call this messy? Wait 'til you see my room.'

They both laughed and then Georgia realised what Zoe had said. Zoe must have too, judging by the way she turned away quickly and asked, 'So, drinks?'

'Oh, yes.' Georgia opened the bar fridge and realised she didn't have much to offer. She didn't know what she'd been thinking, offering her a drink when she didn't actually have anything. 'I don't have a mini bar, so you're limited to water, a milk pod or white wine that Ren left here last week.' She uncapped the bottle of wine and sniffed. 'Smells okay.'

Zoe smiled. 'Wine would be great.'

Georgia poured the wine into two mugs and carried them to the table. When she sat down, Zoe raised her mug and said, 'Cheers.'

'Cheers,' Georgia replied, clinking mugs with Zoe and taking a sip. She squeezed her eyes and shook her head. 'Sorry. Ren hasn't got the best taste.'

Zoe took a sip, closed one eye and pulled a face like she'd just sucked a lemon. 'I don't know what you're talking about. This is top shelf.'

Georgia grinned and dug into her spaghetti. It was as good as the stew had been the night before. 'Molly's a great cook.'

Zoe nodded. 'Means I don't have to.'

Georgia swallowed her mouthful of spaghetti, took a sip of her wine and lifted an eyebrow.

'Sorry,' Zoe said, shaking her head. 'That sounded terrible. I can cook and I do most of the time it's just, I think maybe Molly and Jack worry too much about me sometimes.'

'Oh?'

'I was just out of my teens when Mum and Dad died, so Jack and Molly took care of me. I think they forget sometimes that I'm a grown woman.'

Georgia smiled and nodded. 'I get that. I mean, Ren, who you met the other day, is sort of the same.'

'Oh, really?'

Georgia nodded and took a breath. She hadn't had any intention of telling anyone about Amy's death, but it seemed something she should share, since Zoe was sharing about her parents' deaths. 'My partner, Amy, died a couple of years ago.'

'Shit,' Zoe said, leaning back into her chair. 'I'm so sorry.'

Georgia shook her head. 'It's okay. Really.' Georgia paused to take a sip of her wine. 'Ren thinks it's time for me to move on.'

'What do you think?' Zoe asked.

Georgia looked at Zoe then, really looked at her. Maybe it was the wine making Georgia mellow, but whatever it was, there was a warmth to Zoe's eyes that Georgia hadn't noticed before.

'You know, I don't think anyone's really actually asked me that before,' Georgia said finally.

'Seems sort of important, doesn't it?' Zoe's mouth lifted into a half-smile as she brought her drink to her lips. She let it hover there a moment before she took a sip.

'I guess so,' Georgia replied. She leaned back into her chair, relaxing a little more now. 'I promised Amy I would, but I never thought I'd keep it.'

'Damn dying people asking you to make promises,' Zoe said. She turned the mug around in her hands. 'Dad made me make one too and I haven't kept it, and now it's been taken out of my hands anyway.'

'The workshop?' Georgia asked.

Zoe nodded. 'He told me not to go into the family business, well before he died. I didn't have much of an intention to, but then he and Mum died and Jack needed me. So I quit uni and did my apprenticeship under him. I didn't intend on staying around so long but I really had nowhere else to go.' She let out a breath. 'I guess I just figured here is better than nowhere.'

'So, you're a builder who doesn't like building?' Georgia asked.

Zoe snorted out a laugh. 'I grew into it,' she said. 'And anyway, I love the classes I teach, with the kids. That's what I wanted to do, once Jack got going with the business, but—' She shrugged. 'I guess that's just another pie in the sky thing now.'

'Surely you can find somewhere else?' Georgia asked.

'There's nowhere big enough for my tools and equipment.' Zoe drained her mug and put it on the table. 'And anyway, Jack's hoping your boss is the gateway to bigger things.'

'My boss?' Georgia asked, thrown by the change in direction.

'Rick,' Zoe said.

It took a moment for Georgia's brain to catch up. 'Right. Rick. My boss. What exactly is Jack hoping for?'

Zoe screwed up her nose. 'I probably shouldn't have said anything.' She stood up and picked up her plate, looking around the room. 'Should I rinse this out in the bathroom or something?'

'Leave it. I'll sort it out,' Georgia said, confused at why the conversation had ended so abruptly.

Zoe put her plate back on the table. 'I should probably get going. It's getting late and you need to have a shower and… stuff.'

Georgia sniffed her armpits. 'Are you telling me I smell?' she joked.

'What? No, of course not, I just mean—'

'I was joking,' Georgia said, reaching out and touching Zoe's arm. She realised half a second after she'd done it, and pulled away quickly. 'I'll see you tomorrow then,' she said, hoping she didn't look as embarrassed as she felt.

'Right,' Zoe replied. She turned and walked out the door, Georgia trailing behind her. Zoe stood on the doorstep and there was an awkward silence between them as they just stood there for what seemed like an eternity.

Georgia realised all of a sudden that she was resisting the urge to kiss Zoe. Then she wondered why on earth she was resisting it. Before she could talk herself out of it, she leaned in, intending to kiss Zoe on the cheek. But Zoe turned just at the same moment and appeared to be going to say something, but whatever it was, it was silenced by Georgia's lips finding Zoe's. Zoe didn't pull away, Georgia realised with relief, and when Georgia pulled back, she noticed Zoe had gone slightly pink.

'Sorry,' Zoe said, breathless. 'I, um—' She ran her hand over her the back of her head.

Zoe appeared to be flustered, which Georgia thought was sweet.

'It's okay,' Georgia replied. 'Thank you for dinner. And the chat. It was, nice.'

'Any time,' Zoe said, shoving her hands into her jeans pockets. 'I'll, er, pick you up around eleven tomorrow? For lunch?'

Georgia nodded. 'I'll see you then.' She waited in the doorway as Zoe walked down the driveway to her car. When Zoe got to the end of the driveway, she turned and waved. Georgia waved back and then Zoe disappeared around the corner.

Georgia closed the door and rested her head on it. 'What on earth are you getting yourself into?' she asked herself. She blew out a breath and headed to the bathroom. Zoe had been too polite to say so, but Georgia really did need a shower.

Chapter 35

How had one single kiss almost sent Zoe over the edge? It wasn't even a proper kiss, just a gentle, thank-you-for-dropping-me-home-and-sharing-your-dinner kiss. It was on the lips, though. Zoe touched her mouth with her fingers and then realised what she was doing. She shook herself. Bloody hell, Zoe. Pull it together. It didn't mean anything. Did it?

Oh God, what if it did? What if Georgia was expecting Zoe to kiss her back properly? It'd been so long since Zoe had even been close enough to another woman to even consider kissing her, she was out of practice.

And where did that kiss leave her today? What on earth was she supposed to do when she saw Georgia at the motel? Was she supposed to acknowledge it? Ignore it? Forget it ever happened?

She thought about ringing Molly and asking her advice, but what would she say to her? It was just one very small, very insignificant kiss. But why did it feel like it was so much more?

She pulled into a park outside the motel and pulled the rear view mirror around so she could see herself. She raked her fingers through her hair and tucked a stray couple of strands behind her ear. She took a deep breath and got out of the car. When she arrived at Georgia's door, she took another deep breath to calm the nerves that had started to flutter in her stomach, adjusted her shirt collar, and wiped her hands on her jeans. Then, she knocked. Georgia opened the door and Zoe's throat seemed to close up. She swallowed hard and managed to squeak out a 'Hi.'

Georgia stood smiling at her in a flowing summery dress that showed off her shoulders. It did nothing to calm Zoe's nerves. 'Ready to go?' Georgia asked, closing the door.

'Yep. Yes. Let's go,' Zoe said, turning on her heels and walking off before realising she'd left Georgia trailing behind her. She mentally kicked herself and turned back and waited for Georgia to catch up. What the hell was wrong with her?

'In a hurry?' Georgia asked.

'Don't want to be late for Molly's roast,' Zoe replied, trying to calm herself down. This was Georgia, her client, who she was taking to lunch. It was nothing, really. Businesses took clients to lunch all the time. Not to their brother's house, granted, but still. Nothing except the servo and the pub were open on a Sunday in Elizabeth Creek. But Georgia wasn't just a client anymore. Zoe knew that deep down, no matter how she tried to frame it that kiss last night, intended or not, had changed everything.

As she walked around the back to the driver's side, she took a couple of deep breaths. When she got in, she decided she needed some music to break the tension. She leaned over to the glove box and pulled it open, spilling cassettes onto Georgia's lap and feet.

'Ah, shit,' she cursed, trying to pick up the cassettes.

Georgia scooped up the cassettes off the floor. 'I can get them. Did you want anything in particular?'

Zoe sat back into her seat and shook her head. 'Any of them is fine.' She started the car and drove off as Georgia sifted through the cassettes. Hopefully lunch wouldn't be so awkward.

* * *

By the time they arrived at Molly and Jack's house, Zoe had calmed down. Georgia had maintained most of the conversation on the drive, thankfully, asking questions Zoe could answer without making a fool of herself. Questions like whether Zoe grew up in Elizabeth Creek and where she went to school. Things Zoe already knew the answers to without having to think too hard.

Georgia jumped down from the ute before Zoe had a chance to open her door and said how impressed she was with the house. 'It's based on some old Queenslander designs Jack found in the library years ago,' Zoe explained. 'Built it himself, with Dad's help.'

They walked around the side of the house to the back where Ryan and Josie were chasing each other around the yard with Nerf guns. Zoe led Georgia across the back deck and inside to the kitchen, where Molly gave Georgia a hug, gushed over her dress, and gave Zoe the side-eye and a quick up and down glance at what she was wearing. Normally, she'd wear a pair of old jeans and a t-shirt, but today she was wearing a button-down shirt with a good pair of jeans she normally reserved for special occasions.

As she hugged Zoe, Molly whispered into her ear, 'No need to ask why you're so dressed up.'

Zoe turned her head away, feeling the prickle of heat creeping up her neck. 'I always dress nice for Sunday lunch.'

'Yes, but you don't always iron,' Molly joked, poking Zoe on the shoulder. She turned to Georgia. 'You go on outside with the boys. I need Zoe to help me in the kitchen.'

'Are you sure I can't give you a hand with anything?' Georgia asked, but Molly swatted her outside.

'You're our guest. Go and get Jack to get you a cold drink.'

Georgia smiled at Zoe, making Zoe's heart skip a beat, and then headed outside.

As soon as she was gone, Molly grabbed Zoe by the arm and dragged her into the hallway. 'What on earth is going on? And don't you dare tell me nothing, because look at you.'

Zoe knew she may as well 'fess up because Molly would pull it out of her eventually. 'Georgia kissed me.'

'What? You two kissed?' Molly asked, mouth agape.

'Shh,' Zoe said, peeking around the corner to make sure no-one was listening. 'We didn't kiss, she kissed me.'

'How is that different?'

'Last night as I was leaving her room—'

'Oh, my God, you were in her room? Zoe! Jack's going to kill you!'

'You were the one hinting at me having dinner with her,' Zoe said.

'Dinner, Zo, not sex!'

'Shh! We didn't—' Zoe lowered her voice to a whisper. 'Will you just let me talk?'

'Sorry,' Molly said, and then stood and crossed her arms. If Zoe made her wait any longer, Molly might even start tapping her foot.

'I dropped her home after we finished at the workshop and she invited me in. We ate your spaghetti and we talked. That's it.'

'Talked about what?'

'Stuff. And then when I left, she kissed me.'

'On the mouth?'

Zoe nodded. 'But I'm not sure she meant to.'

'You're not making any sense.'

Zoe had replayed last night over and over in her head so many times, it was hard to know what was real anymore. 'I turned my head and our lips sort of, just…' She pushed the palms of her hands together in an attempt to explain. 'Smushed.'

'Smushed?'

'Smushed,' Zoe confirmed.

'That's it?' Molly asked.

Zoe's shoulders sagged. 'I knew I was reading too much into it.' She went to walk back to the kitchen, but Molly grabbed her arm and pulled her back.

'Did you ask her about it?' Molly asked.

'Of course I bloody didn't. I'm not an idiot,' Zoe said. 'Look, can we just have lunch.'

'You obviously like her, judging by how much effort you went to today,' Molly said, waving her arms over Zoe like she was a prize on a game show. When Zoe didn't answer her, Molly pressed. 'Don't you?'

Zoe hadn't realised it was a question. 'She's alright, I suppose,' she admitted to Molly. It was the first time she'd admitted it to herself.

There was a noise in the kitchen and they both froze. Molly peered around the door, and Zoe peered around Molly. It was Nick, rifling through a drawer. They waited for a moment, and finally he found what he was looking for, a bottle opener, and walked out.

Molly turned back to Zoe. 'Just don't tell Jack about this. You know what Jack thinks about you fraternising with clients.'

'She kissed me, remember?' Zoe said. 'And anyway, this is different.'

Zoe waited for the inevitable warning that she thought was coming, but it never did. Instead, Molly pointed her finger and said, 'Just be careful. I don't want to see you getting your heart broken all over again.'

'But you were encouraging it,' Zoe said, frowning.

Molly waved her away. 'I thought a little fling might do you good.'

'I don't do flings,' Zoe replied.

'I know,' she said, a look of concern clouding her face. Then she shook her head. 'Just, don't be stupid about it.'

'Like I said, there's nothing happening,' Zoe countered.

'Not yet,' Molly said, and pulled Zoe back out to the kitchen.

Chapter 36

Georgia got to see a totally different side to Zoe during lunch. At work, Zoe was serious and professional, but around her family, she seemed to be completely different. Goofy, even, especially with Ryan and Josie. Georgia had laughed watching Zoe chase her niece and nephew around the yard, playing football, and then falling to the ground, letting them tackle her. Zoe was obviously close to her family, that much was true.

Georgia felt a small stab of sadness that she didn't have the same with her own family. An only child, by the time her father died, Georgia hadn't seen him in well over a year. He just always seemed to have other things to do whenever she wanted to see him, so she'd stopped trying. Seeing the way Zoe and her family interacted, knowing that they lost their parents so young, made Georgia realise that she should have made more of an effort with her dad.

'The cottage is coming together,' Molly said, leaning back in her chair cradling her wine glass in two hands.

'It's almost done,' Georgia replied. 'You should come up and have a look. Zoe's done an amazing job.'

Jack smiled. 'I'm glad about that. She can be a bit pedantic about old houses. Loves the history of them.'

Georgia looked across to the yard where Zoe and Nick were teaching the kids how to kick the football off a tee. 'She doesn't like throwing things away, that's for sure.'

Jack chuckled. 'She takes after our old man, except she's a bit more organised than he was.'

'I can't believe you're going to sell it when it's done,' Molly said.

Georgia looked down at her wine glass. She had started wondering the same thing lately. The first time she saw the cottage, run down and sad, she could have gladly bulldozed it and sold the land, but the more it came together, under the careful eye of Zoe, the more she realised what Amy's dream of a much simpler life had meant. 'I know, but I just can't afford to keep it unfortunately.'

'Such a shame,' Molly said, shaking her head. 'I was telling Zoe the other day—'

'Telling me what?' Zoe asked as she skipped up the steps onto the deck and dropped down into a chair beside Georgia.

'That you should buy the cottage,' Molly said.

Zoe glanced at Georgia and rolled her eyes. 'Molly just wants her granny flat back.'

'You live here?' Georgia asked.

Zoe nodded to the shed out the back. 'Converted the back part of the shed a few years ago. In-built baby-sitter.' She winked and turned back to Molly. 'If you wanted to kick me out, you just have to say so.'

Molly tossed a tea towel across the table. 'That's not what I mean, and you know it,' she laughed. 'And anyway, that cottage and the sheds out the back would be perfect for the plans you had for your classes—'

Zoe held up her hand. 'That's all on the back burner now, Mol. And anyway, Georgia doesn't want to hear about any of that.'

'Yes, I do. What plans?'

'They're not important,' Zoe said, throwing Molly a look, but Molly either ignored it or didn't take the hint.

'Zoe had this big idea to create a program for troubled kids,' Molly said.

'That was years ago,' Zoe said, shaking her head.

'Yes, but the cottage would be perfect for it. You should look into it again,' Molly said.

Georgia glanced at Zoe, who was picking the label off her beer bottle with her fingernails. This woman seemed to be full of interesting surprises. There was certainly much more to her than the gruff, bad-tempered builder she portrayed to the outside world. 'That's amazing,' she said. 'Why didn't you?'

'Because I never finished my uni degree is why,' Zoe replied.

Georgia detected a hint of sadness in Zoe's voice, and Jack shifted in his chair.

'Zoe came home to help out in the business when our parents died and never went back,' Jack said.

'And anyway, the workshop's been sold now, so no more woodwork classes,' Zoe added. 'And if Frank wouldn't give me a loan to buy the workshop, he's not going to give me a loan for the cottage.' She drained her beer and stood up and began collecting plates and dishes.

Molly started to do the same but Georgia said, 'I'll help, Molly. You made such a wonderful lunch, at least let me wash up.'

Molly glanced at Zoe as she passed and then nodded at Georgia. 'Thanks.'

'No problem,' Georgia replied as she stacked plates and cutlery and food dishes and carried them inside.

Zoe was rinsing off plates and stacking the dishwasher when Georgia entered the kitchen. She placed the dishes on the counter. 'No wonder Molly agreed to let me wash up. I didn't know she had a dishwasher.' It was an attempt to lighten the mood that didn't work. 'Is everything okay?'

Zoe continued rinsing off plates and stacking the dishwasher and seemed to just want to be alone.

'I'm sorry,' Georgia said. 'I guess I'll leave you to it.' She turned to leave.

Zoe let out a breath. 'It's okay,' she said. 'I'm the one who should be sorry.'

Georgia walked around the bench and leaned back on it. 'It's obviously a sore point.'

'I should get over it,' Zoe said. 'It was eighteen years ago.' She shook her head. 'I just... have you ever had a clear idea of where you were going, and then, just had it ripped from under you?'

Georgia nodded. 'I have. That's what Amy's death was. She had these grand plans for us and then she died, and the plans died with her.'

'And then you just get stuck,' Zoe said, picking at her fingernails.

Georgia hadn't thought about it that way before. She'd never considered her life without Amy until she was gone. All her plans for the future had Amy in them, and for the first time she realised that maybe she'd been just going through the motions over the last few years. She could see so much of herself in Zoe, and although her plans weren't anything like Zoe's, she understood completely what it was like to have them ripped away. She reached out and took Zoe's hand and gave it a squeeze.

'Maybe it's time to rethink your plans,' Georgia said. Maybe it was time they both did.

* * *

Something had definitely shifted between them, Georgia was sure of it now, and on the ride back to her motel, she felt more relaxed than she had in a long time. She hadn't asked anything more about Zoe's youth program plans, figuring that if Zoe wanted to tell her about them, she'd do it in her own time.

The electricity zoomed between them as they walked to Georgia's room, she could feel it. They were close enough to touch but didn't, and just the thought of taking Zoe's hand, like she'd done without thinking at Molly and Jack's, sent a wave of excitement coursing through Georgia's body. It was all she could do to stop herself from touching Zoe again.

'Thank you for today,' Georgia said when they reached her room.

'Any time,' Zoe replied. 'Molly loves having people over.'

'I could tell,' Georgia said with a smile.

Zoe leaned on an awning post, smiling back at her, looking so kissable it was all Georgia could do to stop herself. And then Zoe stood up and stepped forward, closing the distance between them.

'Do you… may I…?' Zoe said, her face inching closer to Georgia's and before she could finish her sentence, Georgia stepped forward and pressed her lips to Zoe's.

Zoe's arm snaked around Georgia's waist, pulling her closer until their bodies touched from hips to chest and Georgia reached up and threaded her fingers through Zoe's hair. This was what Georgia intended the night before, this warm, soft, slow kiss that sent shivers from her head to her toes.

Zoe stopped abruptly and rested her forehead on Georgia's. 'I should get going.'

'Really?' Georgia asked, breathless.

'I've got some more stuff to do at the workshop.'

'I could come and help,' Georgia offered.

Zoe smiled and squeezed Georgia's hand. 'No offence, but I think you'd just be a distraction right now.'

Georgia shook her head. 'None taken.'

Zoe stepped back. 'I'll pick you up in the morning?' she said as she backed away.

'I'll be here,' Georgia replied. She leaned on the awning post and watched Zoe walk away. 'Those jeans,' she said to herself, 'are definitely not work jeans.'

Chapter 37

Zoe and Georgia fell into a routine over the next few days, with Zoe picking Georgia up from her motel each morning, complete with breakfast rolls and coffees, and then teaching Georgia how to use the various power tools. It meant that when Nick was off practising his dancing and strutting for the Mister Elizabeth Creek competition, work didn't slow down too much.

Georgia had upped her flirting game too, stealing winks and kisses. Zoe was sure Nick would catch them at some point but she needn't have worried. He was absolutely clueless. Zoe was standing on a trestle nailing chamfer to the wall when Georgia walked past and pinched her on the butt, and Nick was too busy measuring up the next piece of timber to even see it.

Zoe jumped and turned around. 'Hey! I could've nailed my hand to the wall.'

Georgia just winked and kept walking.

'You'll keep,' Zoe called after her, and then had an idea. She handed the nail gun to Nick. 'Finish off these ones. I'm going to the loo.'

She jumped down off the trestle and headed to the shed, detouring via her ute, where she took her dad's fake finger from the glove box. In the shed, she pulled the tomato sauce bottle from the lunch box and squirted a bit into her hand. When she got back to the Nick, she said, 'Can you go grab some more nails?'

Nick handed Zoe the nail gun and dropped down to the ground. Zoe waited until he'd turned the corner and then she set up her prank. She rubbed the tomato sauce on the end of the fake finger and then held it onto the board. As she shot a nail into it, she yelled and swore as loudly as she could.

Nick was the first to come running. 'You okay boss?'

Zoe nodded. 'Yeah, just got my finger, that's all.'

Nick took one look at the board with Zoe's fake finger nailed to it, oozing tomato sauce, and went white. 'I'll go get Georgia,' he said, stumbling away.

Zoe laughed at Nick's squeamishness. She'd have to remember not to rely on him if she ever had a real accident.

Georgia came barrelling around the corner and stopped dead at the bottom of the trestle. Nick hung back, his ashen face turning green.

'Nick said you had an accident,' Georgia said, climbing up onto the trestle. 'What happened?'

Zoe pointed to her finger, trying to look like she was in pain. 'Got my hand in the way.'

Georgia pulled a face. 'Nasty. Does it hurt?' She reached out to touch it but Zoe batted her away. 'Sorry,' Georgia said. 'What can I do?'

'Grab my hammer out of my belt. We'll need to pull it out,' Zoe said, hoping her wincing was convincing.

Georgia nodded. 'Nick? Go grab the first aid kit.'

Zoe glanced at Nick, who was now bent over, his head between his knees. She tried desperately not to laugh. 'I don't think he can hear you.'

Georgia climbed down from the trestle. 'I'll go get it myself. Be right back.'

As Georgia rushed away, Zoe couldn't help herself. She burst out laughing. Georgia spun around. 'Are you okay? Nick, I think she's going into shock.'

That made Zoe laugh even harder. She pulled her hand from the wall and wriggled her fingers. Nick almost fainted.

'You two...hilarious,' Zoe wheezed, doubled over with laughter.

'Are you okay?' Georgia asked.

'Fine,' Zoe replied. 'Perfectly fine. It's a fake, see?' She dipped her finger in the tomato sauce and licked it. 'Tomato sauce.'

Nick almost threw up, sending Zoe into hysterics. He stood up and disappeared around the corner.

Georgia, on the other hand, glared at Zoe, her arms crossed across her chest. 'I can't believe you thought that was funny.'

Zoe took a few deep breaths to stop herself from laughing. When she saw the look on Georgia's face, she wondered if she'd made a huge misjudgement about her sense of humour. To her relief, a smile spread across Georgia's face and she shook her head and laughed.

'You're so going to pay for that,' she said. 'But first, I think I better look after Nick.'

Zoe giggled to herself as she pulled the nail out of the fake finger and wiped the tomato sauce off the chamfer. That reminded her, it was almost time for lunch.

Chapter 38

Zoe called the day off early, which Georgia was pleased about. It meant they got to spend some time together at Zoe's place taste-testing Molly's baking for the show. Molly had decided to enter three categories – scones, custard slice and vanilla cupcakes.

They'd eaten their way through three scones and two cupcakes each and were just about to try Molly's custard slice.

'This,' Zoe said as she divided the creamy slice into two and handed one to Georgia, 'is the best custard slice you'll have in your life.'

'That's a pretty big statement to make,' Georgia said, picking up her slice and taking a bite. She closed her eyes and moaned. 'Oh. My. God.'

'See?' Zoe said, grinning. 'You can't even get them that good at the bakery.'

Georgia swallowed and took another bite. 'If this doesn't win, there's something seriously wrong.'

'The custard slice category is pretty fiercely contested,' Zoe said. She took a bite of her slice, the custard oozing out of the sides. She caught it with her hand. 'First time Molly's been able to enter, that's how fierce the competition is.'

'Imagine being a judge,' Georgia said, delicately popping the last piece of her slice into her mouth.

'You'd get very fat, I reckon,' Zoe said, standing up. 'I need something to wash this down with. Do you want anything?'

'I'd love a coffee,' Georgia replied. While Zoe was in the kitchen, she took the opportunity to check out the photos Zoe had scattered around the TV cabinet. It was easy to pick Zoe out. She had a broad grin and fly-away hair and seemed to be always doing something rather than sitting still. In one photo, she had her mouth open, apparently mid-sentence, while in another, she was sitting with a man Georgia presumed was her grandfather, and was staring intently at something he held in his hands, one knee bent up in front of her, the other leg dangling off the bench.

Zoe handed Georgia her coffee and pointed to one with Zoe sitting on a bench in front of a wall of records, her arm around her dad's waist. 'Pop and Dad used to help out at a local community radio station.'

'Really?'

Zoe took a sip of her coffee and nodded. 'Dad was into ham radios and stuff when he was a kid. Thought he was going to be a radio star.'

Georgia smiled. 'He looks like he loved it.'

'He did,' Zoe replied. 'Had to give it up when Pop got crook. Got his fix by calling up the talk-back shows though.'

It sounded to Georgia like letting go of your own dreams to be part of the family business seemed to run in the Jennings family. She figured she probably didn't need to say that out loud. She took hold of Zoe's hand and squeezed.

'Is that why you keep all those cassettes in your car?'

Zoe smiled. 'They're copies of Dad's old play lists. Some of them even have him talking on them. Stuff he pre-recorded for the late night spots when he couldn't make it in.'

Georgia's heart softened. 'Do you listen to them?'

Zoe swallowed and took in a long breath. 'Once a year,' she replied, and Georgia knew when that was without having to ask.

There was an awkward silence between them. Georgia wasn't sure what to say next, but thankfully, Zoe broke it by pointing to another picture. This one was of her Pop, Dad and Zoe and Jack, the two kids sitting proudly on a timber bench.

'That's the workshop,' Zoe said.

Georgia sipped her coffee. 'Looks exactly the same.'

Zoe nodded. 'Pop had it all set up perfectly. The only thing Dad added was a kid-sized work bench in the back for me and Jack to muck around on when we were there.' She let out a breath. 'I'm going to miss that place.'

'It must be hard to let it go,' Georgia said, quietly.

Zoe nodded and let out a breath. 'There's so much history in that old place. I'm just glad I still have all the old workbenches and tools. I just wish I could find somewhere to put it all.'

'What about the cottage?' Georgia asked.

Zoe screwed up her nose and shook her head. 'There's no way I can afford something like that now it's done up.'

'I could help you get the finance,' Georgia offered. 'That is my job.'

Zoe let go of Georgia's hand and dropped heavily onto the lounge. Georgia followed her over and sat beside her.

'I'd be happy to have a look,' Georgia pressed. 'Just to give you an idea. I actually think Molly's right. It would be perfect for your classes and if you wanted to set it up for that youth camp idea.'

'Like I said the other day, that idea is dead,' Zoe said, her voice turning a little harder.

Georgia knew she'd hit a sore point, so she decided to let it go. 'I'm sorry. I just think it's a great idea, that's all, and obviously your family does too.'

Zoe snorted out a breath. 'Jack needs me in the business right now. There's no time for pie-in-the-sky stuff.' She drank her coffee and looked across the room.

Georgia wondered if Zoe was thinking about her parents, and whether things might have been different if they were still alive. Things would have been different for Georgia if Amy was still alive, that was certain. For a start, there was no way Georgia would have been falling for her builder. That thought jolted her, surprising her. Was she falling for Zoe because she missed Amy so much, she just wanted the company? Or were the feelings she was starting to have for Zoe real?

She grabbed Zoe's hand and squeezed. Zoe gave Georgia a sad smile. A sense of melancholy seemed to settle itself over the room.

A knock at the door made Zoe pull her hand away. She jumped up and opened the door to find Jack on the porch.

'Molly's got some more scones she wants you to try,' he said.

'I don't know if I can fit much more in,' Georgia said.

Jack chuckled. 'She's got another batch of cupcakes in the oven too, so don't think the scones are the last of it.'

Georgia looked at Zoe who was still standing by the door. She raised her eyebrow. 'I'm keen if you are?'

'We won't need dinner if she keeps baking like this,' Zoe replied.

Jack grinned. 'That's what I'm hoping.' He wheeled away and Georgia and Zoe followed.

'How do you stay so thin with all Molly's cooking?' Georgia asked as they walked across the yard to the main house.

'Just good genes,' Zoe shrugged.

Georgia pinched Zoe on the butt. 'Good jeans alright.'

Chapter 39

The week had gone fast, especially now that Zoe and Georgia seemed to be spending much more time together outside of the build. After work each day, they'd end up at Zoe's place, kissing and joking and getting to know each other, before they'd have dinner with Jack, Molly and the kids.

For his part, Jack seemed to be pleased that Zoe and Georgia were finally getting along, and if he knew something was going on between them, he didn't say. Molly certainly wouldn't have mentioned it to him that was for sure.

Although Zoe was starting to really fall for Georgia, she was determined to take things slowly. She was extremely conscious of Georgia still missing Amy, and she didn't want to push their relationship any faster than Georgia was comfortable with.

Molly had been asking for updates on their relationship but Zoe had been stonewalling her, not wanting to jinx it or put a name to it. Who knew what would happen when the next week was up? She hoped Georgia would stick around a bit longer, and she didn't want to think about her going back to the city and never coming back, even though that was a distinct possibility.

All Zoe knew was that for right now, she was enjoying renovating the cottage, and she was pretty sure Georgia felt the same way.

She crawled out from under the cottage, pushing a mound of timber and debris in front of her. She'd been cleaning out what felt like a hundred years of rubbish under the floor space so Simmo could install new pipes. She picked up a pile to take to the overloaded skip bin and began shoving bits in wherever it would fit. She picked up the last piece of timber and was about to toss it in when something caught her eye.

She brushed the dirt off to reveal some routed letters, and when she rinsed the timber off under the tap, it revealed the words 'Hill House'. The letters were hand-carved by the look of the tool marks and Zoe realised that this must be the original name of the cottage. She dusted herself off and rushed through the back door to find Georgia standing in the middle of the floor where the kitchen was going in the next day, her hands on her hips.

'Hey,' Zoe said. 'Check this out.' She showed Georgia the sign. 'Looks like this might have been the original cottage name.'

'The cottage had a name?' Georgia asked.

'Most old places do,' Zoe replied. 'I'd say the Hill family owned this one originally, or it's because the house is built on a hill.'

Georgia glanced at the sign. 'How original,' she said with a smile.

'You'll have to come up with a name for this one,' Zoe said.

'Can't we just use that one?' Georgia asked.

'It's not the same cottage, but I can clean this up and paint it and put it somewhere...' She glanced around the room. 'Maybe in here, to show the history of the place.'

'If you want,' Georgia replied with a shrug. She seemed distracted.

'What are you doing in here? I thought you were cleaning windows?' Zoe asked.

'I was,' Georgia said. 'And then I came in here and realised that I just couldn't picture it.'

'Picture what?' Zoe asked.

'The kitchen,' Georgia replied, waving her hands in the air. 'I just can't see how it would work.'

'That's a bit of a problem considering it's getting installed tomorrow,' Zoe said. 'And anyway, it's not like you'll be cooking in it, if you're selling it.'

Georgia pulled a face and rolled her eyes.

'Okay,' Zoe said, scratching her chin. 'Make me a sandwich.'

Georgia looked horrified. 'I beg your pardon?'

'If you want to know whether the kitchen layout works, you need to know how you'd use it,' Zoe explained. 'Make a sandwich.'

Georgia looked around at the tape on the floor. 'What sort of sandwich?'

'What does it matter?' Zoe asked.

'It matters,' Georgia said, 'because if you want Vegemite, I have to go to the pantry.'

'The fridge,' Zoe corrected her.

Georgia's eyebrows shot up. 'No way! You keep your Vegemite in the fridge?'

'Don't you?'

'I do not,' Georgia replied with mock disgust.

'Vegemite's too easy,' Zoe said. 'How about a ham, cheese and tomato?'

'Really?' Georgia asked.

Zoe crossed her arms. 'What's wrong with that?'

'It's a bit boring, isn't it?' Georgia said.

'There's nothing wrong with ham, cheese and tomato,' Zoe shot back. 'It's a classic.'

'I suppose so,' Georgia said. 'But have you ever tried chicken and pesto, with sun dried tomatoes? Much nicer, especially if you make it with focaccia.'

'We don't have focaccia,' Zoe said.

'How do you know? Is this your kitchen or mine?' Georgia asked, one eyebrow raised.

Zoe resisted the urge to roll her eyes. 'Just make the damn sandwich.'

Georgia snorted out a breath but moved around the pretend kitchen, commentating her movements as she went. Zoe noticed the subtle change in language Georgia used, from being distant from the build at the beginning to referring to 'her' fridge, 'our' cutlery and 'my' kitchen. She wondered if Georgia was considering keeping the cottage. She wouldn't be the first person to fall in love with a renovation project that was meant to be for profit, but she wondered what Rick Wheeler would think about that. As for worrying about what fake sandwich she was making though, that was next level.

'Cheddar or Swiss?' Georgia asked, holding her hands out like she had cheese in each of them.

'What do you think?' Zoe asked.

'Well, I'd say cheddar, since you're obviously—' she stopped mid-sentence and glanced at Zoe, one eyebrow quirking up. 'Traditional,' she finished. 'But I'm going to give you Swiss, just for something different. You'll love it, I promise.'

Zoe rolled her eyes and held her tongue. How had such a simple exercise turned into something so bloody complicated? After making her pretend sandwich, Georgia stopped all of a sudden and put her hands on her hips, glancing around.

'What's wrong now?' Zoe asked.

Georgia glanced up. 'Where do we keep the plates?

'Oh for crying out loud,' Zoe said, throwing her hands into the air.

Georgia mimed pulling out a drawer and placing the invisible sandwich on an invisible plate.

'Done?' Zoe asked hopefully.

'Almost,' Georgia replied.

Zoe almost hated to ask, but she did anyway. 'What now?'

'Do you want your sandwich toasted? Because I'll need to know where we keep the sandwich press,' Georgia replied.

If it wasn't for noticing the corners of Georgia's mouth twitching up into a smile, and that smile making Zoe's heart beat just a little bit faster, Zoe would've told Georgia to stop being so painful. Instead, she said, 'I'm fine with untoasted.'

Georgia smiled. 'Do you want me to cut it into triangles or rectangles?'

'Just give me the damn sandwich,' Zoe replied, surprising herself by sticking out her hand and accepting the invisible plate.

They stood there smiling at each other for a moment, and then Georgia crossed her arms and said, 'Well?'

'Well what?' Zoe asked.

'Aren't you going to take a bite?'

Zoe rolled her eyes, but she laughed in spite of herself along with Georgia. 'Was there anything else you needed my opinion on?' she asked.

'That was all,' Georgia replied, still smiling.

Zoe stole a kiss and then turned and walked away.

'Where are you going?' Georgia asked.

'Some of us have work to do,' Zoe replied, grinning as she skipped down the back steps. 'And don't forget to clean up the kitchen.'

Chapter 40

On Friday after lunch, Georgia sat outside having a cool drink in the shade of one of the sheds, watching the show crews set up in the distance. The Ferris Wheel went up earlier in the day, the afternoon sun reflecting off the carriages, and Georgia could make out some other rides going up nearby. She wondered what it would look like at night.

Nick had been backwards and forwards from the cottage during the week, and had most afternoons off so he could practice whatever it was he was doing for the Mister Elizabeth Creek competition. Georgia was looking forward to seeing what it was all about on Saturday night. She hadn't been to a show in years, not since Amy had gotten sick.

The Ekka in August was one of Amy's favourite things. She was such a big kid at heart, it was hard not to get pulled in to her fun and adventurous spirit. Amy probably would've loved to go to the Elizabeth Creek Show. Georgia was surprised to find that that thought didn't make her sad like it once would have. Nick had asked her to go and watch him tomorrow night, and when Zoe confirmed she and Jack and his family would be there, it was a no-brainer. It would be nice to have some fun for a change. She stood up and carried her chair back to the shed to find Zoe on the phone.

Zoe smiled at her and nodded and when she finished the call, she said, 'Want to be an apprentice for a bit longer?'

Georgia grinned. 'Why not?'

'We've got to go over to the showgrounds and fix the door on the caller's box,' Zoe said.

'What do you need me to do?' Georgia asked.

'Hold my tools,' Zoe winked, kissing Georgia on the cheek.

'I guess I can do that,' Georgia grinned.

Zoe unlocked the old wooden door at the back of the grandstand and pushed it open. She walked in and started up the stairs but Georgia didn't follow.

'Are you sure it's safe?' Georgia asked.

Zoe came back down one step and ducked her head so Georgia could see her through the doorway. 'It's fine, trust me.' She held out her hand and wiggled her fingers. 'Pass me the toolbox.'

Georgia handed Zoe the toolbox and followed her inside into the darkness. The wooden ladder creaked as they climbed, giving Georgia the feeling it was far older than it looked on the outside.

'Watch your head,' Zoe said as they reached the top. She pulled on a cord and a low-hanging light came on, illuminating the cramped space.

Georgia ducked through the doorway at the top of the stairs and stood and watched while Zoe unlocked a wooden shutter and pushed on it. It didn't budge.

'Probably just needs some grease,' Zoe said, grunting as she gave the shutter one last shove.

Georgia watched as Zoe went about her business, greasing and loosening the hinges until the shutter opened and closed easily. 'That's got it,' Zoe said, apparently satisfied. She opened the shutter all the way up and dragged the bench seat forward and sat down. She patted the seat and Georgia slid in beside her.

'It's a bit tight,' Zoe said. 'It's only really meant for one person.'

'It's cosy,' Georgia agreed, sliding over so their legs were touching. She placed her hand on Zoe's knee.

Zoe leaned forward. 'It's a great view from up here, isn't it?'

Georgia watched the show workers going about their business below them, setting up rides and food trucks and games.

'Dad used to bring me up here when I was little,' Zoe said. 'My grandfather built this place.'

'Did he?'

Zoe nodded. 'Every inch of it, and Dad did the upgrades and now Jack and I do the maintenance.'

'Impressive,' Georgia replied. 'Do you get to come up here often?'

'Outside of fixing stuff? Once a year. On the anniversary of their deaths.'

Georgia turned, surprised. 'But, Jack said you go camping every year.'

Zoe smiled and shook her head. 'Jack thinks he knows a lot of things.' She leaned her elbows on the window and rested her chin on her hand. 'This is the place I feel closest to all of them.'

Even though Georgia didn't have a place like this to feel closest to Amy, she could certainly relate. 'So how do you get away with it?'

'Get away with what?' Zoe asked.

'Sneaking up here every year with no-one knowing.'

Zoe's mouth turned up into a sly smile. 'I park the ute at the work shed and carry my swag down. That's why I go late at night. Everyone's in bed.'

'And no-one would question your ute being parked at work,' Georgia said. 'Clever.'

'Thank you,' Zoe replied.

'And you never thought to tell Jack and Molly?'

'They've never asked,' Zoe replied.

'Fair enough,' Georgia said.

There was a noise at the bottom of the ladder, and Nick's voice carried up from below. 'You up there, Boss?'

'Yeah,' Zoe replied.

'Can you come give us a hand with the stage?' Nick called.

Zoe rolled her eyes. 'Sure can. I just have to drop Georgia back first.'

'Oh, hey, Georgia.'

'Hey, Nick.'

'We're in the main pavilion,' Nick called.

'I'll be there in a bit,' Zoe replied to Nick. She stood up and closed the shutter. 'The minute they see the ute, everything needs fixing.'

'Well, you do seem to be Ms Fixit,' Georgia replied with a smile, and climbed back down the ladder.

As Zoe locked up, Georgia said, 'I can give you a hand if you like.'

'Are you sure?'

Georgia shrugged. 'I don't have any other plans, and I am supposed to be your apprentice this week so…'

Zoe grinned. 'Okay then.'

As they walked to the pavilion, Georgia asked, 'Do you think I might get to do more than just pass you the tools?'

Zoe laughed. 'Don't get too far ahead of yourself.'

Chapter 41

Zoe grunted as she loosened a bolt on a leg of the main workbench. Nick had brought some mates over to help move them after they'd finished at the show grounds, but they were way too heavy to move whole, so on Saturday morning before she headed to the show, Zoe had set about pulling them apart. It was a shame to have to pull them down, but there was no other way to move them.

'Righto,' she called to Nick, and they lifted the top off the bench and carried it outside and slide it on to the back of the ute. While Zoe tied it down, Nick retrieved the legs and slid them on top.

'Can't believe that's it,' Nick said as he caught the end of rope Zoe tossed him.

Zoe didn't reply. She still had a few days yet to clean the old workshop before the new owners took it over and she was trying not to think about closing those old barn doors for the last time.

She was tightening a knot on a rope when Jack rolled up beside her.

'We need to talk,' Jack said and then rolled away into the workshop.

'You're right to finish this?' Zoe said to Nick.

Nick saluted and Zoe followed Jack inside. 'What's up?'

'You just can't stay away from trouble, can you?' Jack said, his voice low.

'What are you talking about?'

Jack raked his hands over his face. 'You were seen, Zo, in bloody public.'

Zoe shook her head. 'Do you want to catch me up or am I just going to have to guess?'

'You and Georgia,' Jack said. 'Getting cosy at the show grounds. Do you have any idea—?'

Zoe held her hands up. 'Wait a minute. Georgia and I weren't getting cosy at the show grounds, and even if we were, what business is it of yours?'

'I need this job to work, Zoe, you know that. I can't have you jeopardising it for a bloody fling with the same woman who could be the difference between our business going bust or not.'

'I doubt Georgia holds that much power, Jack, and even if she did, whether Georgia and I are seeing each other is none of your damned business.'

'It is my business,' Jack said, getting animated. 'Because I pay your damned wages.'

'My love life is nothing to do with your business,' Zoe hit back. 'Whatever happens with the business is on you. You're the manager.' She turned on her heels and walked out.

'She'll break your heart, you know that,' Jack called but Zoe ignored him.

When she got to the ute, Nick was trying to look busy, so Zoe knew he'd heard every word. She reefed open the driver's door and climbed into the seat.

Nick got into the passenger side and put on his seat belt. As they drove off, Nick said, 'So, you and Georgia, hey?'

Zoe glared at him. 'If you say anything about me and Georgia,' she said through gritted teeth. 'You'll be walking to the show grounds from the edge of town.'

Nick put his hands up. 'Don't want to talk about it. Got it.'

* * *

Zoe was still smarting from her argument with Jack when she arrived at the show grounds later that afternoon. It wasn't just that Jack would believe gossip about his own sister, but also that he still just saw her as someone to boss around. The lines often blurred between them since she'd started working for him, and she'd never felt like she should walk away from the family business more than she had than this morning

She bent down closer to the display, eyeing off the craftsmanship of the whittling category in the carpentry section. This was her grandfather's forte, apparently. She had no memory of him, except for the smell of pipe tobacco and aftershave because he'd died when she was five, but she had a carving the size of her hand of a kangaroo he'd made her when she was born.

Whittling was a talent she hadn't been able to master. Not that she'd tried much or often. Slicing her thumb open with a pocket knife when she was ten was enough to put her off it for life, though she sometimes wondered whether she'd have learned if she'd had her grandfather to teach her.

She made her way around the display until she found the boxes her carpentry class had made and smiled to herself at the distinction ribbons her students had received. She wondered where on earth she was going to move her classes to once she'd moved from the old workshop. The cottage renovations hadn't left her much time to find somewhere else but she'd have to start looking sooner rather than later.

'Are any of these yours?' came a voice from behind her. Zoe turned to see Georgia standing there, smiling, and she immediately relaxed, the argument with Jack forgotten. She looked more like Georgia in her jeans and linen shirt that showed a little of her collarbone. She'd had her hair up the last few weeks while she worked at the cottage, so it was nice to see her with it down again.

Georgia gave her a quick peck on the cheek, and Zoe looked away quickly.

'My kids,' Zoe said, indicating the cabinet, and then seeing the confusion on Georgia's face, she clarified. 'The carpentry class you met the other day.'

'Oh, right. So you don't enter anything?' Georgia asked.

Zoe shook her head. 'Not anymore. Jack keeps telling me I should get back to joinery but I don't really have the time. What about you? Any hobbies you've entered into a show?'

Georgia shook her head. 'No, but my grandmother was a Grand Champion chocolate cake baker in Brisbane.'

'Is that right?' Zoe said, impressed. 'I love a good chocolate cake.'

'Me too,' Georgia replied. 'Pity Gran took her winning recipe to the grave.'

'Mum did that with hers too,' Zoe said. 'Wish I'd paid more attention while she was alive, but I was more interested in being out in the workshop on jobs with Dad.'

'You're lucky you got to spend time with your dad,' Georgia said. She sidled up to Zoe and peered into the display case. 'Mine wouldn't let me near his work.'

'Really?' Zoe asked.

Georgia nodded. 'No daughter of his was going to go near a building site. He'd probably have a fit if he saw me now.'

A voice over the PA system announced the Mister Elizabeth Creek competition was due to begin in half an hour.

'We should go find Nick,' Zoe said. 'Knowing him, he'll be nervous. He'll feel better once he sees we're there to watch him.'

They found Nick over by the judges' table. He was wearing his best tan jeans, his black boots were buffed to a dull shine and he had a dark blue jacket slung over his shoulder. He raked his hands through his hair and even from a distance, Zoe could tell something was wrong.

'Nick,' Zoe called.

Nick turned and when he saw Zoe and Georgia he rushed over in a panic. 'Zoe! I don't know if I can compete,' he said, the words rushing out.

'Why not?' Zoe asked.

'Tara's in the toilet throwing up. I told her not to go on the Gravitron until after the comp, but she said she'd be fine,' Nick said. 'If I can't find someone to walk out with me I'll be disqualified.'

'What about that friend of yours from school?' Zoe asked. 'Phoebe whatsername?'

Nick rolled his eyes. 'She's partnered with Mitchell Drummond.'

Zoe knew all about Mitchell Drummond. The way Nick told it, Mitchell thought he was all that and a bag of chips. Which was exactly why Nick didn't like him. 'You want me to kneecap Mitchell so Phoebe has to go with you?'

Nick looked hopeful. 'Would you?'

'No, I would not,' Zoe laughed. 'I was joking, Nick, bloody hell.'

Nick's face dropped.

'I could do it,' Georgia offered.

Nick and Zoe both turned to look at Georgia, surprised.

'It's just walking down the catwalk with you, isn't it?'

'Yeah, and the dance a bit later but Tara might be right for that,' Nick said.

'Are you sure?' Zoe asked.

Georgia shrugged. 'There doesn't seem to be much to it. Besides, Nick's obviously gone to a lot of trouble to get dressed up and look so handsome.'

Nick blushed and dropped his eyes to the floor. 'You don't have to,' he mumbled.

'We don't want you disqualified,' Georgia said. 'Go and tell them you've found yourself a partner.'

Nick grinned and rushed back to the judges' table.

Zoe leaned into Georgia and whispered, 'I think he's got a crush on you.'

Georgia swatted her away.

'And I don't blame him,' Zoe said, giving Georgia's hand a squeeze.

Nick gave them a thumbs up from the judges' table and when he made his way back to them, he was grinning from ear to ear. 'They said you can be my partner,' he said. 'Except you have to wear a dress.'

Georgia's face dropped. 'Where am I going to find a dress at short notice?'

Zoe pulled out her phone and dialled Molly's number. As she put it to her ear she said to Georgia and Nick, 'Wait here. I'll be back in a minute.'

Chapter 42

Georgia smoothed the dress over her stomach and regarded herself in the mirror as Molly zipped her up at the back. 'Thanks for this,' she said, as Molly moved around in front and looked her up and down.

'Knowing the organiser of the fashion parade has its advantages,' Molly replied as she adjusted the strap on Georgia's shoulder. She nodded and grinned. 'I think that'll do nicely.'

Georgia sucked in a breath and let it out. The dress wasn't anything too spectacular. It was just an ordinary sun dress, really, but it fit well enough. She hoped Nick would be okay with it.

The voice over the PA requested all couples to make their way to the back of the stage. 'Better get going,' Molly said.

'Yep,' Georgia replied. She tucked a stray piece of hair behind her ear and followed Molly out of the dressing room and into the hall to the back of the stage.

Nick's eyes grew wide when he saw her. 'Wow,' he said.

Georgia glanced around at the dressier gowns on the girls standing around back stage. 'I hope this is okay,' she said. Those girls had to be half her age, which made Georgia nervous. She reminded herself that this was for Nick and that she was a grown woman who didn't care what anyone else thought.

The MC announced the first couple, who disappeared around the backdrop and onto the stage, and soon, Nick and Georgia were standing at the bottom of the steps, waiting their turn. Nick offered Georgia his arm and she slipped her arm into his and let him lead her onto the steps ready to go on stage. Nick's name was called and Georgia took the next step up but Nick stood stock still.

'What's wrong?' Georgia asked.

Nick just shook his head.

Stage fright, Georgia thought. The announcer called his name again and Georgia knew she had to do something. She grabbed Nick by the shoulders and made him look at her. 'Follow my lead.'

Nick just nodded. Georgia took him by the hand and pulled him onto the stage. She virtually had to drag him along the stage to get his feet moving. They stopped half-way and Georgia lifted Nick's arm up. 'Spin me,' she whispered out of the side of her mouth.

'What?'

'Spin,' Georgia hissed again.

Nick got the hint but instead of letting Georgia spin, he did a pirouette and the crowd clapped and whistled. Although it wasn't what Georgia meant, for some reason it loosened him up a little and as they walked to the end of the catwalk, Georgia felt him relax beside her. She decided to go with it.

'I'm going to bend you over,' Georgia said as they reached the end.

Nick's head snapped around and he looked horrified.

'Like the end of a dance,' Georgia clarified. 'Like you should do for a girl, but opposite.'

'Oh,' Nick nodded.

Georgia hoped he understood. Dropping him on stage would probably be disastrous for his chances. As they reached the end of the stage, Georgia fell a step back and then, hoping Nick would catch on, pulled him back to her so their hips were touching. His face went as red as a beetroot, and she took one hand in hers and put the other in the small of his back, she thought he might explode from the embarrassment. A knot formed in the pit of her stomach but there was no turning back now.

She bent Nick over backwards and to her surprise, he totally went with it, throwing his head back and flicking his hair out, before she pulled him back up to thunderous applause from the crowd.

Nick took control of their walk back up the catwalk, strutting the whole way, giving a salute across to Zoe and her family when he caught sight of them where they were standing off to the side.

They exited the stage on the opposite side they went up on and Georgia started. 'Nick, I'm so—'

'That was fantastic!' Nick gushed, lifting Georgia into a hug and then putting her back down, apologising.

'I thought I embarrassed you,' Georgia replied, relieved.

'No way! I just, wow, did you hear them when we did the—' he mimed Georgia's move at the end of the catwalk. 'They went nuts!'

'What's next?' Georgia asked.

'Oh, um,' Nick scrunched up his nose. 'All us guys have to go back out together while they judge our outfits.'

'So, you don't need me for that?'

'Don't think so. But I might need you later for the dance, if Tara's still, you know, throwing up her hot dog.'

Georgia pulled a face and tried not to picture that scenario. 'Just let me know. I'm going to find Zoe. Come and get me if you need me.'

'Thanks,' Nick said.

Georgia pushed her way through the crowd hanging around near the stage and found Zoe and her family right where they'd been before. She touched Zoe lightly on the arm.

Zoe turned and then smiled in recognition. 'Nick's going to be talking about that for weeks, you know. You've probably got yourself a fan for life now.'

Georgia grinned. 'I was happy to help. Has Tara turned back up yet?'

Zoe shook her head. 'She's in the St John's first aid rooms. She should be okay for the dance later but we'll have to wait and see.'

The crowd clapped and cheered as the last of the couples left the stage and the MC came back out. Georgia felt Zoe stiffen beside her and she realised that he was the same man she'd seen her arguing with at the pub. She glanced sideways at Zoe, whose mouth had changed from a smile to a thin line, her jaw muscles working overtime. What was it with that man?

Georgia leaned in to talk into Zoe's ear. 'Hey, I want to check out more of the show. Want to show me around?'

Zoe relaxed a little and turned her head slightly to Georgia. 'Can we go after the outfit judging?'

Georgia nodded. 'I should probably go change out of this dress anyway.'

'You could stay in it,' Zoe said. 'It, ah, looks good on you. Molly's got good taste. And you might be needed for the dance later.'

Georgia smiled. 'I don't want to mess it up. I'll be back in a sec.'

When she got back stage, Georgia stood and watched as Zoe cheered and woof-whistled when Nick sauntered down the catwalk. The obvious affection she had for Nick was sweet. Molly was right about her not being as tough as she let on. Despite their rocky beginning, Georgia was beginning to see a nicer, softer side of Zoe, and she had to admit, she liked it.

Chapter 43

Zoe met Nick backstage after the outfit judging to find him chattering away to Tara, who was still looking a little worse for wear. The nerves obviously gone, during his second stint on stage Nick strutted around playing up to the crowd, showing off his fitted pants by patting his butt and taking off his jacket and slinging it casually over his shoulder. He even tossed his hair around like he was in a shampoo commercial, making the crowd completely lose it. It was a side of him Zoe had only seen when he'd had a few drinks and she was happy to think it was Georgia who'd drawn it out of him.

Georgia, in that dress, that shifted lightly as she walked down the catwalk. Her hair down, tossed casually over her shoulders. She looked like she'd stepped out from the pages of one of Molly's magazines. Just the thought of it made Zoe's insides dance.

She punched Nick on the arm. 'You bloody show off,' she joked. 'You did good.'

Nick beamed. 'Thanks, Boss.'

'How long before the dance part?'

Nick glanced at his watch. 'About an hour. Can you let Georgia know that Tara's going to do it?'

Zoe glanced at Tara, who was looking a little pale but smiling through whatever she was feeling at that moment. She wasn't sure Tara was up to being pulled around a dance floor with Nick, but she didn't question him. It meant she'd get to spend some time with Georgia.

'You can tell her yourself,' Zoe said, nodding over Nick's shoulder.

'Tell me what?' Georgia asked as she walked over and stood by Zoe's side. She'd changed back into her jeans and shirt, and was pulling her hair up into a ponytail.

Nick looked uncomfortable and, Zoe noticed, Tara seemed to stand up a little taller. 'Tara's going to be okay for the dance,' Nick said.

'Oh,' Georgia replied. 'Are you sure?'

Nick nodded and as he opened his mouth to reply, Tara spoke first.

'Thank you for being Nick's partner, but I'm okay now.'

'Okay then,' Georgia said. If she detected the hint of jealousy coming from Tara, she didn't say anything.

Instead she said to Zoe, 'I guess we can go and have a look around, if you haven't got any other plans?'

'Nope. I'm all yours,' Zoe said.

'Right, well, good luck with the dance,' Georgia said, hugging Nick and nodding at Tara.

Zoe gave Nick a cursory slap on the shoulder. 'Let me know how you go.'

Nick saluted and then turned and walked back into the crowd with Tara.

As Zoe and Georgia headed back outside, Georgia said, 'Was it just me or was Tara claiming her territory?'

'I thought so too,' Zoe replied. 'Can't blame her really.'

Georgia glanced sideways at Zoe, her eyes glinting.

'That dress was pretty spectacular,' Zoe admitted. 'So what do you want to do first?'

'Eat,' Georgia replied. 'I'm starving.'

'Deep fried show food coming up,' Zoe said, and when Georgia linked her arm into hers, Zoe couldn't wipe the smile off her face.

After consuming the customary Dagwood Dog and wandering around Side Show Alley, Georgia suggested they have a go on the Dodgem Cars.

'Are you sure?' Zoe asked, eyebrows raised.

'Yes, why?' Georgia asked.

'You don't seem to be the Dodgems type.'

Georgia crossed her arms. 'And what type is that?'

'Too nice,' Zoe said with a shrug.

'You don't think I'll be happy to smash you in a Dodgem car?' Georgia scoffed.

'You'll have to catch me first,' Zoe joked.

'You're on,' Georgia replied, pulling Zoe over to the ticket counter.

Zoe climbed into her car, waggling her eyes at Georgia, who poked out her tongue in return. She clicked on her seat belt and looked across at her competition. There were a couple of kids getting into cars, who Zoe resolved to go easy on, and as she glanced back across to say something to Georgia, she saw Frank Dickson climbing into a car across the other side of the arena. She took a deep breath and told herself not to even think about him and to focus only on Georgia and having fun.

Georgia got in the first two hits since she started behind Zoe, and Zoe tried to avoid the tangle of kids in the corner to chase Georgia down. In her peripheral vision, Zoe saw a car coming fast directly across the arena. As she turned the corner, she giggled when Georgia got herself stuck between two kids, but then Frank came hurtling in from behind, hitting Georgia's car, causing her head to snap back.

Zoe narrowed her eyes and as she waited for the jam to clear, Frank glanced around and when his eyes settled on Zoe, his face turned from laughing to horror and as soon as he was free, he took off, with Zoe in pursuit. She zoomed past Georgia, who was giggling as a little girl t-boned her, narrowly avoided a collision with a boy who had managed to get himself spinning backwards, and closed in on Frank.

As she cut a corner at the end of the arena, Frank turned at the other end and Zoe saw her chance. She spun the steering wheel hard and took off through the middle, her eyes focused only on Frank. He turned another corner and Zoe turned with him. Just as he straightened up, Zoe ploughed into him, hard, lifting the back of the car and jerking his head sideways.

He put his foot down and his car shot forward, straight into the path of another car. He turned and scowled at Zoe. She gave him the finger and spun her steering wheel to back away from the wall and get back on track.

When the ride was over, Georgia grabbed Zoe's hand. 'What was that all about?'

'What?' Zoe asked.

'You know what,' Georgia replied. 'I saw you arguing with that same man at the pub a few weeks ago, and I saw your reaction to him in the pavilion.'

'That was Frank Dickson,' Zoe replied.

'The Frank Dickson that sold the workshop on you?' Georgia asked.

Zoe nodded. She let out a breath, realising how childish she must have looked in front of Georgia. 'Sorry. I saw him hit you and I just saw red.'

'The only thing I'm sorry about is that you didn't tell me about him. I would've hit him too if I'd known.' Georgia smiled.

Zoe kissed Georgia on the forehead. 'Thanks.'

'We should go find a seat somewhere,' Georgia said. 'Won't the fireworks be on soon?'

'I've got a better idea,' Zoe said. 'Come on.'

Chapter 44

As they drove the now familiar roads out to Carramar, Georgia turned to look at Zoe, confused. 'We're going to the cottage?'

'Best place to see the fireworks, I reckon,' Zoe replied. 'There's a clear view from your yard, and no-one will spill drinks down your back.'

The creek was still running when they drove over it, even though they hadn't had a storm in a few days, but it had gone down enough to be running under the new causeway. When they arrived at the cottage, Zoe backed the ute up so they were facing the house.

While Zoe set the swag and sleeping bag out in back of the ute, Georgia took in the view. The predicted storms had moved further north, leaving the full moon just visible behind some lingering clouds. The sounds of the show were muted across the valley but the lights were colourful and bright. Georgia had to admit, it was pretty spectacular from where she was standing.

'Okay. You're all set,' Zoe said, climbing into the tray of the ute and helping Georgia up.

Georgia propped herself up and got comfortable. 'This is amazing.'

'Told you,' Zoe replied, grinning. She shuffled down onto the swag and leaned in so their shoulders were touching. She checked her watch. 'I reckon we've got about a half hour before they start.'

Georgia laced her fingers into Zoe's. 'I wonder how Nick went?'

'If he wins, we're sure to find out about it pretty quick,' Zoe replied with a laugh.

'He looks up to you, you know,' Georgia said.

'So he should. I am his boss,' Zoe replied.

'No, I mean, I think he sees you as his big sister,' Georgia said.

'Yeah, well, he and Dallas have had a bit of a rough life. It's good seeing him do so well.'

'You seem to be so good with kids. Did you ever think about having any of your own?' She felt Zoe's chest rise and then fall as she let out a breath.

'Never found the right person to have them with, I guess,' Zoe said. 'What about you?'

It was Georgia's turn to let out a breath. 'Amy had a daughter. Paige. She's fifteen now.'

'Wow.'

'Yeah. Amy's biggest regret was not fighting for her,' Georgia said, the sadness of that memory bubbling up again. 'She, we, hadn't seen Paige since she was four. Amy's ex-husband moved interstate and wasn't overly supportive of her relationship with me.'

'Do you have any contact with her now?'

Georgia shook her head. 'The last time I saw her was at the funeral. I gave her a quick hug but with her father hanging around, we didn't get a chance to talk.' She shifted so she could lay her head on Zoe's chest. 'Paige is part of the reason I have to sell the cottage.'

Zoe shifted her weight under Georgia's head. 'Oh?'

'Amy's family, they fought me for the estate.' Georgia blew out a breath. 'I need to sell the cottage to pay my legal fees.'

Georgia felt Zoe's arms tighten around her. She closed her eyes and swallowed the lump that had formed in her throat.

Georgia felt Zoe's lips brush her forehead. 'I'm sorry about that.'

Georgia snuggled in tighter. 'Thanks.'

Zoe was silent for a long while. 'You didn't think you might want to keep it?'

Georgia shook her head. 'It just reminded me of all the promises Amy and I made to each other before she died. To be honest, I'm not entirely sure how I feel about it anymore, now that I'm here.'

'Fair enough,' Zoe replied. She squeezed Georgia's hand. 'I get it.'

Georgia relaxed again. 'Thank you.' She was glad Zoe had understood. When she'd arrived in Elizabeth Creek, the history she had with the cottage didn't matter, but the closer she got to Zoe, the more she wanted to be completely honest with her.

'Look,' Zoe said, nodding towards town. 'The lights are dimming. The fireworks must be about to start.'

Georgia snuggled back into Zoe's chest and watched as the lights went out on the Ferris Wheel and the first of the fireworks shot into the sky. It exploded in a shower of pink sparks, and was quickly followed by more.

Zoe ran her fingers up and down Georgia's arm, making Georgia shiver.

'Cold?' Zoe asked.

'No,' Georgia replied. She glanced up and realised that Zoe wasn't watching the fireworks. She had her eyes fixed firmly on Georgia. 'Hi,' Georgia said.

'Hi,' Zoe replied, leaning closer. For a moment they both sat looking into each others' eyes until Zoe finally closed the distance between them, her lips warm and soft on Georgia's. As the fireworks went off in the distance, Georgia and Zoe made fireworks of their own.

* * *

Zoe wondered if Georgia could feel the electricity zapping between them as they lay side-by-side in the darkness. They'd missed most of the fireworks, and Zoe didn't regret a second of it. She reached up and pushed a stray hair off of Georgia's face and tucked it behind her ear.

'Are you ready to go back yet?' Zoe asked.

Georgia shook her head.

Zoe smiled. 'Me neither.'

When Georgia reached up and cupped Zoe's cheek with her hand, Zoe thought she might combust. Georgia lifted her face closer and it was all the invitation Zoe needed. She closed the space between them, pressing her lips to Georgia's, and when she felt Georgia's hands grip hers tighter, she knew that whatever she'd been feeling about them, together, the last few days, Georgia was feeling it too.

Georgia snaked her arm around until her hand was touching the small of Zoe's back, pulling her closer. Zoe obliged, shuffling over until she could slip a leg between Georgia's, their bodies touching at the hip.

They kissed, long and slow, sensual, turning Zoe inside out with pleasure. She pulled away to catch her breath.

'Are you sure about this?' she asked.

Georgia nodded in reply.

'I'm okay if you want to go slow,' Zoe said. Her body was aching to get close to Georgia but after what she'd shared about her last partner tonight, she didn't want to push Georgia too far too fast.

'Stop talking and kiss me,' Georgia whispered, tugging at Zoe's shirt.

Zoe didn't need to be asked twice. She reached back and pulled her shirt over her head, and as Georgia's hands slid over her back and unclipped her bra, Zoe lowered herself down and lost herself in the warmth of Georgia's embrace.

Chapter 45

It had been years since Georgia had woken in someone's arms, and although the back of the ute wasn't the most comfortable place she'd ever been, Zoe's chest made up for it. She wiped her mouth with the back of her hand, feeling Zoe shift underneath her. She lifted her face to look at Zoe, who was smiling down at her, a lot more awake than Georgia was.

'How long have you been awake?' Georgia asked, rolling onto her back and stretching her arms over her head.

'A little while. I didn't want to wake you up,' Zoe replied. She lifted herself up onto one elbow and rested her head on her hand. 'Sleep okay?'

Georgia closed her eyes and sucked in a breath, letting it out slowly. 'Better than I have in a long time.'

Zoe raised an eyebrow and grinned at her. Then she kissed Georgia on the forehead and sat up. 'I don't know about you, but I'm dying for a coffee.'

'Should we get one at the cafe?' Georgia asked.

'Won't be open yet,' Zoe replied. 'But my place is.'

Georgia grinned. 'Are you hoping for a repeat performance?'

Zoe grinned. 'That wasn't my intention, but my bed's a bit more comfortable than the swag.'

'I could use some sleep,' Georgia said. 'Since we didn't get a lot last night.'

As they drove back into town, Georgia thought about last night, the memory of Zoe's lips on hers, Zoe's hands on her bare back, sending a wave of butterflies from her head to her toes. She reached across and lay her hand on Zoe's knee.

Zoe glanced at Georgia. 'What's that look?'

'I just had a great night last night,' Georgia replied.

Zoe laced her fingers into Georgia's. 'Me too.'

Georgia never thought she could be with anyone after Amy, but she'd realised last night when she was telling Zoe about Amy and the plans they'd had for the cottage, the cancer and the aftermath, that she didn't feel sad anymore. She'd felt unburdened for the first time in years and Zoe had been a big part of that.

It had been an emotional night, for the both of them. She'd just felt so connected to Zoe last night, that sleeping with her seemed the most natural thing in the world. It felt like she'd released the tension that had been building since Amy had died. Everything that

Georgia had been dealing with, Amy's death and the fall out with her family, the fight over Amy's estate and then deciding what to do with the cottage had all melted away last night.

Georgia thought about what Zoe had said last night about selling the cottage. Was she selling it for the right reasons? She wasn't sure anymore.

Chapter 46

Zoe moved the armchair a little to the right. 'Better?' she asked.

Georgia cocked her head and then finally, nodded. 'Perfect.'

Zoe wiped her sweaty hands on her jeans. 'Fantastic. Just the beds to go.' She walked up the hallway with Georgia in tow and turned into the first spare bedroom.

She pulled a shifter from her tool belt and got to work setting up the cast iron bed frame. With Georgia's help over the last two days, they'd almost finished setting up the house ready for Ren and Rick's arrival later that day.

They pulled the plastic off the mattress and lifted it onto the bed. Georgia flopped down onto it. 'Comfy,' she said. 'Want to see?' She waggled her eyebrows and Zoe shook her head and laughed.

Georgia beckoned Zoe with her finger and blew a kiss.

Zoe shook her head. 'You're irresistible, you know that?'

Georgia smiled seductively. 'So I've been told.'

Zoe climbed onto the bed and leaned up on one elbow, pushing Georgia onto her back. She lowered her face to Georgia's hovering just close enough for their lips to brush before Georgia grabbed the back of Zoe's neck and pulled her down. Zoe grinned as they kissed, her hand slipping under Georgia's shirt, up over her side and cupping her breast.

Georgia pulled back. 'You look hot.'

'Why thank you,' Zoe replied.

'I think you should take off your shirt,' Georgia said, her voice low and husky.

Zoe sat up and pulled off her shirt, tossed it to the floor, and lowered herself back down onto Georgia.

Georgia's hands were hot on Zoe's back and just as she undid the clasp on her bra, a car door slammed outside.

'Shit!' Zoe jumped off the bed, snatching her shirt from the floor.

'They weren't supposed to be here for hours yet,' Georgia replied, fixing her hair and adjusting her clothes. 'Stay here.'

Zoe did as she was told. She fastened her bra and tugged her shirt over her head and ran her fingers through her hair. She cast her eyes around the room and settled on the box of bed linen in the corner. She needed to look busy. As she tossed pillows and a doona onto the bed, she heard voices in the hallway.

'Zoe? You remember Ren?' Georgia said.

Zoe spun around and plastered on a smile. 'Sure. Hi. How was the trip out?'

'Great, thanks,' Ren replied.

Rick stepped forward and thrust out his hand. 'Rick.'

For some reason, Zoe felt like she had to wipe her hands on her jeans before she shook hands with him. 'Nice to meet you, Rick.'

Rick cast his eyes around the room. 'Nice job you've done,' he said.

'Wait until you see the kitchen,' Georgia said, ushering Ren and Rick out. As she left, she gave Zoe a quick wink.

Zoe grinned, feeling like a teenager again, getting caught making out by her Mum. She switched her focus back to the bed linen, vowing to finish what Georgia had started as soon as they got the chance.

* * *

Later, as Zoe was ferrying rubbish to the skip bin outside, she overheard Georgia and Ren talking in one of the bedrooms. She wouldn't have paid too much attention, but she heard her name mentioned. She lingered near the window.

'I told you a fling with Zoe would be good for you,' Ren said.

Georgia didn't say anything. Instead, she laughed.

'Didn't I tell you that?' Ren asked.

'Yes, you did.'

'Are you glad to get it out of your system?'

'I mean—' Georgia said and then Rick's voice interrupted.

'Get what out of your system?'

'Nothing,' Georgia replied.

'Right,' Rick said. 'Women's business. I get it.'

There was a silence for a moment and then Ren's voice again. 'You can tell me about it later.'

'There's nothing to tell,' Georgia replied.

'Whatever,' Ren said. 'I just hope it's gotten you out of your Amy funk.'

'Can we just get the house finished?' Georgia said.

Zoe set her jaw. A fling. That was what Georgia had thought of their… whatever it was they had. Zoe had just been a way for Georgia to forget her dead partner. Well, that was fine with her. Georgia would be going back to the city anyway at the end of the week, so it was just as well Zoe found out now.

She tossed the rubbish into the skip bin and stomped back to the cottage. 'I'm heading off,' she called from the back door, trying to keep the anger out of her voice.

Georgia's head appeared from behind the island bench. 'Everything okay?'

'Fine,' Zoe replied. 'You've got things covered here, so I'll leave you to it. I've got to finish cleaning the workshop before I hand back the keys.'

Georgia started walking across the room. 'Are you sure? I can come and help if you like?'

'I said I'm fine,' Zoe snapped. The surprise on Georgia's face made Zoe's heart twinge. 'You've still got plenty to do here. I'll be fine.'

'We'll catch up later then?' Georgia asked.

'I'll see how I go,' Zoe grunted. And with that, she turned and left, determined not to think about Georgia for the rest of the afternoon.

Chapter 47

Something wasn't right with Zoe, Georgia could feel it. She'd heard the terse tone in Zoe's voice when she'd left the cottage earlier. Whatever it was, Georgia was determined to find out.

She'd managed to fob Ren off, leaving her with Rick to decide on photo locations so she could go into town and talk to Zoe. She drove past her house, but her car wasn't in the driveway, so she drove to the workshop. Zoe's car was parked at an odd angle in the car park. It looked like she'd parked and gotten out in a hurry.

Georgia parked her car and got out, poking her head around the door way. Zoe was up the back sweeping the floor. She looked up but didn't even acknowledge Georgia. She just went back to sweeping.

'Is everything okay?' Georgia asked as she walked inside and stood nearby.

'You tell me,' Zoe replied, continuing her sweeping.

'Can you just stop and talk to me?' Georgia said.

Zoe stopped sweeping and looked up. Georgia could see the anger and pain written across Zoe's face.

'What is going on?' Georgia asked. 'You left the cottage in a hurry.'

'Why should you care? I'm just a fling,' Zoe said.

'No, you're not,' Georgia replied, stepping forward.

Zoe stepped back. 'That's what you said at the cottage, isn't it?'

'I never said that,' Georgia said.

'Bullshit, I heard you,' Zoe replied.

Georgia felt her face flush. The conversation she'd had with Ren. 'What you heard wasn't everything,' Georgia said. 'I was trying to throw Ren off.'

'You're a liar, Georgia,' Zoe said. 'You lied about who you were, you lied about your job, why wouldn't you lie about us?'

'Well, you were perfectly fine with me being the project manager when you were trying to get into my pants to help out with your brother's business.' Georgia didn't know why she'd said it, but as soon as the words were out, she regretted them instantly. She hadn't come to argue with Zoe, and she certainly hadn't come to hurt her. She took a step forward and reached out but Zoe pulled away.

'Look,' Zoe said, her jaw tightening. 'You said yourself, you don't want to give up your apartment.

You're obviously still very much in love with Amy, and I get that. I really do. But I can't compete with her and I shouldn't have to.'

'You're not competing with her,' Georgia replied.

'Are you sure about that?' Zoe asked, cocking her head. 'Amy's dead, Georgia. She's not coming back.'

Hurt bloomed in Georgia's chest and tears pricked her eyes. 'Don't you think I know that?'

'Well stop acting like you owe her something,' Zoe said. 'I know what it's like to lose someone you love, to feel like you can't move on.'

Georgia snorted out a laugh. 'You're the last person to talk.'

Zoe crossed her arms. 'What's that supposed to mean?'

'You get on your high horse about moving on and doing my own thing and here you are, eighteen years later, working in a business you never wanted to be in, being angry about not getting to do what you really want to do and never doing anything about it.'

'Don't you throw this back on me,' Zoe spat back.

'Why not? If Jack's business goes bankrupt, what are you going to do then?'

Zoe didn't say anything for a long time. Finally, she took her broom and turned and walked away. When she got to the bottom of the stairs she said, 'I think you need to go and do what you have to do, and I have to get this place clean.'

Georgia just stood and watched as Zoe walked up the stairs to the mezzanine floor. She had no more words and no more fight in her. How had this day that had started so well ended so badly? Her heart heavy, she turned and walked back out to her car. There was nothing left for her at Elizabeth Creek, now that the cottage was finished, and whatever it was she'd had with Zoe was done too.

She'd go back to her motel, pack her bags and head back to the city and leave Ren and Rick to deal with the cottage.

Chapter 48

Two days after Georgia's departure, Zoe had been dragged out to Carramar by Jack so they could talk about the upcoming auction with Rick and Ren. Rick and Jack had been doing most of the talking about the market and potential buyers, and although Zoe was trying to pay attention, she was acutely aware of Ren's eyes boring into her from across the table. It took all her strength to ignore it.

'So we're good to go then,' Rick said, relaxing back into his chair. 'I have to say, Jack, you've done an amazing job.'

'This is all Zoe,' Jack said, slapping Zoe on the back. 'I know I'm biased, but she's the best damn builder I know.'

Rick smiled and nodded. 'Well, I'm sure we'll have buyers climbing over themselves to grab this little piece of paradise. Right, Ren?'

Ren nodded and plastered on a smile. 'Sure.'

'So I guess all that's left to talk about,' Rick said, 'is that business proposition you floated, Jack.'

'Sure,' Jack said.

Before he could get started, Zoe pushed her chair back and stood up. 'If you don't need me, I'm going to head home.'

'This concerns you too,' Jack said.

'You're the boss,' Zoe said. 'Whatever it is you're working on, I'll be fine with.'

'Sorry, Rick, can you just give us a minute?' Jack said.

Rick nodded and he and Ren stood up and walked outside. When they were gone, Jack lowered his voice. 'This is an important business decision, Zoe. It's going to affect both our futures.'

'That's why you should be dealing with it,' Zoe said. 'You're the one with the business brain, not me.'

'You're a partner in this business. You should be having a say,' Jack said.

'Am I, Jack? That's news to me.'

'Lower your voice,' Jack said. 'What the hell is that supposed to mean?'

Zoe leaned in and angry-whispered through gritted teeth. 'You never ask me what I think about anything to do with the business, Jack. Why on earth would you start now?'

Jack sat back in his chair. 'This is about Georgia, isn't it?' He shook his head. 'I told you getting involved with her was a bad idea.'

'It's got nothing to do with Georgia,' Zoe replied, though she knew that wasn't exactly the truth. All she could think about the last few days was Georgia bloody Ballantyne.

'It's got everything to do with her,' Jack said. 'You get all caught up in some girl who's just going to walk away and then get all bloody upset about it when they leave.'

Anger rose up in Zoe's chest and her hands balled into fists. They'd been teenagers the last time they'd come to blows, and it took all her strength to not want to hit him now. She took a step back and shook her head, willing herself not to say all the things that were running through her head. She turned and walked away. When she got to the back door, she stopped. 'Maybe it's me who should've left.'

Jack called after her but she ignored him as she stormed out to her ute, reefed open the door and got in. She closed her eyes and lay her head on the steering wheel. Georgia had really done a number on her.

When she opened her eyes, she saw Ren glaring at her in her rear-vision mirror. She revved the engine and tore down the driveway, kicking up dust, but didn't care. The further away from the cottage she could get the better.

Chapter 49

The noise in the cafe was giving Georgia a headache, and it took all of her concentration to listen to what Ren was saying. Apparently, Jack and Zoe were now working in conjunction with Rick's company, which was exciting for them, she supposed, but she wasn't sure how someone as laid back as Zoe would take working for someone like Rick. He was all business and pushed his employees hard. She couldn't imagine Zoe not telling Rick where to shove it if he got on her nerves, but then again, she knew how loyal Zoe was to Jack so maybe she'd curb her temper.

Zoe's loyalty and love for her brother and his family was a big reason Georgia fell for her. The way she genuinely cared about people, even if she wasn't close to them, had softened the hard edges she portrayed to the world. Georgia loved that side of Zoe. She missed that Zoe.

Georgia turned her attention back to Ren, who was now detailing the ins and outs of the market research she and Rick had done. Her stomach turned into knots. It was all getting so real now. In just a few days, the cottage would no longer be hers and the burden it had been on her life would be gone. For some reason, she just couldn't get excited about that.

A waitress arrived, asking to take their orders. Ren ordered a latte and a piece of custard slice. Georgia ordered the same. She told herself she just couldn't decide on anything else, but she really knew it was because the custard slice reminded her of Elizabeth Creek.

'I doubt it'll be as good as Molly's,' Ren was saying. 'But for some reason, custard slice is all I've been able to think about since I tried hers. I'll have to remember to get her recipe when I'm out there this week.'

Georgia grunted a reply.

'Are you sure you don't want to be there when the hammer goes down?' Ren asked. 'You said you wanted closure.'

'The further away from that place I am on auction day, the better,' Georgia replied.

Ren put her hand over Georgia's. 'Are you absolutely sure you want to sell the place? We can hold off on the auction if you want more time to think about it.'

Georgia shook her head. 'What's done is done.'

'Nothing's finalised yet, George. If you're having second thoughts—'

'No second thoughts,' Georgia replied. 'I just don't need to be there to see it go, that's all.'

'If you say so,' Ren said in that tone Georgia knew full well meant she didn't believe a word Georgia was saying. She ignored it.

'So, how's it going being back at work after all that time off?' Ren asked.

Georgia shrugged. 'Same as always.' She didn't have to look at Ren to know her eyes were boring right into her.

Finally, Ren said, 'Look, George. We've been friends for a long time, and as your best friend, I feel it's my duty to tell you when you're being a total and utter idiot.'

Georgia snorted out a breath but didn't reply.

'I know what's going on, you know,' Ren continued.

'Nothing's going on,' Georgia replied.

'That's the problem, isn't it?'

'What's that supposed to mean?' Georgia could hear the sulkiness in her voice and she hated it.

'Ever since you got back from Elizabeth Creek, you've just been moping around your apartment. This is the first time I've managed to get you out in public—'

'I go out in public,' Georgia retorted.

'Going to work is not going out in public,' Ren said. She paused while the waitress placed their food on the table, and when she was gone, she said, 'You're miserable, and I hate seeing you like this.' She took a sip of her coffee, pulled a face and stirred in two sugars. 'It's worse when it's your own stupid fault.'

Georgia scoffed. 'My fault, is it?'

Ren looked up. 'Who's do you think it is?'

Georgia didn't answer. As far as she was concerned, it was no-one's fault. She and Zoe just weren't made for each other. 'It was never going to work.' Georgia prodded at the froth on her coffee.

'You never gave it a chance to,' Ren said.

'She was the one who ended it,' Georgia replied.

'And you let her,' Ren said. Her face softened. 'Look, George, I know you miss Amy terribly, and it's obvious how much you like Zoe.'

Georgia opened her mouth to say something but Ren put her hand up to silence her.

'You can still love Amy, and fall in love with Zoe, you do realise that, don't you?'

'I don't love Zoe,' Georgia said, her voice almost a whisper.

'Maybe not yet,' Ren said. 'But I have no doubt that's where you were heading before you walked away.'

'I didn't walk away, Zoe ended it,' Georgia said, her voice defiant now. If Zoe hadn't told Georgia to leave, she would have stayed. She was sure of it.

'You have to fight for these things,' Ren went on. 'You fought for Amy when you first started dating, remember that? Her husband gave you so much grief those first few years, and you fought because you knew Amy was worth it.'

'That's not fair,' Georgia said.

'What's not fair is you giving Zoe up without a fight. What's not fair is you walking away from a good person, a good life, because for some reason you think you needed Amy in it for it to work. Well, guess what, George? Amy's not here and she won't ever be, and it's not fair on her to keep making excuses for why you can't move on with your life and find someone to share it with.'

And there it was. The truth bomb that Ren had delivered hit Georgia right where it hurt. Amy wasn't coming back. Not ever, and Georgia knew she couldn't change that. And no matter where she lived, Amy would never be there.

Georgia took a bite of her custard slice. It was nowhere near as good as Molly's. She pushed her plate away. She'd never be able to eat a custard slice again.

Chapter 50

Zoe stood in the empty workshop and looked around. She'd never seen it empty before and for the first time, she realised how big it must have felt to her when she was little. She tossed the keys up in her hand and caught them. She'd been holding off handing them over to Frank, but there was no more putting it off.

She pulled the barn doors closed and as she locked them up, a car pulled in to the car park behind her. She turned to see Ren emerge from a red SUV.

Zoe started walking to her ute. 'I've got stuff to do.'

'So have I,' Ren said. 'Like setting the record straight and finding out why you'd let Georgia just walk away. She's been moping around her bloody apartment for weeks.'

Zoe hadn't spoken to Georgia since she'd left. The fact that she was moping was news to her. As far as she knew, Georgia was much happier back at home in the city. Zoe opened the door. 'Don't you come here playing the protective best friend when it's partly your fault.'

'How's it my fault?' Ren said.

'You told her to have a fling with me to make her get over Amy,' Zoe said.

'That is true, I admit that,' Ren replied.

Zoe huffed out a breath. At least Ren was willing to admit that. 'Great. Did you even think how I'd feel about it? Being treated like some throw-away relationship that got Georgia over whatever bloody depression she was feeling?'

'But that's not what happened,' Ren said. 'Obviously it was more than that, judging by the way Georgia's been acting.'

'Look, Georgia's obviously better off in the city, and that's fine with me.'

'Didn't you just hear what I said?' Ren asked. 'I said Georgia's not fine.'

'What am I supposed to be doing about that?' Zoe asked. 'We had a fling, your words, and that was it. Now we're both getting on with our lives.'

Ren shook her head. 'Are you that stupid?'

Zoe pulled a face.

Ren rolled her eyes. 'I'm trying to tell you that she's fallen for you,' Ren said. 'I haven't seen her like this in a long time. Not since she fell for Amy.'

Zoe didn't want to hear any more of this. Georgia was back in the city, and that was her choice.

'I have to go,' Zoe said.

As she slid into the seat, Ren called, 'You've made a huge bloody mistake, Zoe. And if you don't fix it, you're going to regret it.'

She and Georgia would never have worked. Even if Georgia had stayed, at some point, she would've gotten bored with life in Elizabeth Creek, just like all the others, and then Zoe would've been left to pick up the pieces again. No. It was better they ended things when they did before it had gotten too serious.

She double-parked out the front of Frank's office, reefed open the door and stormed in past Nellie Roebuck at reception. She ignored the looks from Frank's work colleagues and when she got to Frank's desk, she threw the workshop keys at him.

'Happy now?' she said and turned on her heels and walked out.

* * *

Zoe was finishing up her third beer when she heard a noise at the bottom of the caller's box. She pulled the cord for the light and peered down the hole. She was surprised to see Molly half way up the ladder.

'What are you doing here?' Zoe asked.

'I know this is where you hide out when you're sad,' Molly said as she climbed into the room and dusted off her hands. 'And on the anniversary.'

'How did you—?'

'You can be stupid sometimes,' Molly said, but her voice was filled with affection.

'You're the second person to tell me that today,' Zoe said. She handed Molly a beer and took one for herself.

Molly sat down on the seat beside Zoe and uncapped the bottle. 'What on earth are you doing?'

'Drinking,' Zoe replied.

'You know what I mean,' Molly said. 'I've been talking to Ren and apparently Georgia's a mess.'

Zoe rolled her eyes. So Georgia had gone from moping to a mess. 'I don't want to talk about it anymore.'

'Well you might not, but I do,' Molly said. 'And you're going to listen.'

Zoe knew it was pointless to argue, so she leaned out onto the window sill and prepared herself for Molly's lecture. Once Molly was done, Zoe would agree to disagree and then go home and not think about it again.

'You need to get your head out of your backside, Zoe Jennings,' Molly said.

Zoe laughed in spite of herself.

Molly whacked Zoe lightly on the arm. 'I'm serious. You had a good thing with Georgia. Why on earth would you throw that away?'

'She would've left eventually,' Zoe replied.

'You're sure about that are you?'

Zoe didn't reply.

'She said to you 'Zoe, even though I like you a lot, I'm going to leave in a few months time and break your heart', is that it?'

'No,' Zoe conceded.

'Or maybe it's you who decided you'd get in first,' Molly said, her voice softening.

'Better for both of us,' Zoe grunted. 'It wouldn't have worked out anyway.'

'Oh, you know that, do you?'

'Yes.'

'How? Did you ask her?'

Zoe huffed out a breath. 'Jack warned me this would happen.'

'Oh, Jack did. I see. Did you ever consider your brother could be wrong?'

Zoe turned her head to look at Molly.

'Zoe, I love your brother dearly, and he wants the best for you but what he thinks is best and what is actually best are two very different things,' Molly said.

'What are you talking about?'

'Jack doesn't want to lose you, Zoe. He thinks he can't run that business without you, and it got worse when he had his accident.'

'But he's the smart one,' Zoe replied.

Molly laughed. 'You'd think so, wouldn't you?' She took a drink from her bottle. 'He's got a great business brain but for some reason, maybe because he feels like he wants to protect you, I don't know, but whatever the reason is, he's afraid you're going to leave and he's going to lose you, just like you both lost your parents.'

Zoe shook her head. 'I'm not going anywhere.'

'You almost did, remember?' Molly said.

Zoe leaned back on the seat and looked up at the ceiling. 'Elke.' Elke had come to town on a working tourist visa nearly eight years ago, and Zoe had fallen head over heels for her within weeks. They made plans to go travelling, and every time Zoe got close to booking tickets, Jack pleaded with Zoe to do just one more job. In the end, Elke got sick of waiting and left town without so much as a goodbye. She'd broken Zoe's heart, and Zoe had thrown herself into the business to forget. 'That makes much more sense now.'

Molly put her hand on Zoe's shoulder. 'So you can see why Jack wouldn't want you starting anything with Georgia.'

Zoe nodded.

'You can't keep putting your life off for his, Zoe,' Molly said. 'He's never going to do what he needs to do as long as you're protecting him.'

'I'm protecting him now?' Zoe asked.

'You're his crutch,' Molly said. 'As long as you're part of the business, he can say what he likes about going big, and never really do anything about it because he tells himself he needs to keep you employed.'

'I didn't realise that,' Zoe said.

'Well, now you do,' Molly replied.

Zoe blew out a breath. 'What a bloody mess.'

'Yes,' Molly agreed. 'The question is, what are you going to do about it?'

Zoe took a long drink from her beer. 'I guess I'm going to have to talk to Jack.'

Chapter 51

Georgia threw her keys onto the hall table and dumped her bag onto the floor beside it on the way to the kitchen. She poured herself a scotch and carried it into the lounge room, where she kicked off her shoes and stood looking out the glass windows. She had an overwhelming sense of deja vu. She took a sip of her drink and let out a breath.

The last few weeks had been hell. She hadn't realised just how much she didn't like her job until she had to go back after her time off. She certainly hadn't realised how much work she'd done to make her boss look good until she'd walked back into her office and found a mountain of work only half-completed. Was it stupid to miss sanding and painting as much as she did? She laughed at the absurdity of even thinking that.

There was a time that looking out across the river to the horizon would have made her relax, but the last few weeks that she'd been back, seeing the mountain range in the distance just made her miss the hills of Elizabeth Creek.

She knew it was stupid and she knew she should get over it, because the cottage was due to go to auction in a few days, but she'd wondered more than once what would have happened if she'd decided to keep the cottage instead of the apartment.

But that would mean walking away from her job and if she did that, what would she do? Ren had tried on more than one occasion to make her think seriously about keeping the cottage and making it a bed and breakfast, but what did she know about the accommodation industry?

And besides, going back to a small town like Elizabeth Creek, where everyone there probably knew what had happened between her and Zoe was the last thing she wanted to do. Zoe had made it very clear she wanted nothing to do with Georgia, and they hadn't spoken to each other since the argument in the workshop. Georgia couldn't blame her really.

She drained her glass and padded into the bedroom and sat cross-legged on the floor near the bed. She pulled a box from under it and opened it. Amy's memory box.

Georgia had asked Amy once why she kept all the seemingly random stuff she did.

'To remember,' Amy had replied.

'That's what memories are for,' Georgia had teased, but then Amy had told her the story about her grandmother, her mind and memories lost to dementia. Of how the smallest things could trigger a long lost memory for her, and it became clear to Georgia why Amy was determined to bring so many trinkets into their home.

In the end, it wasn't dementia that had claimed Amy but cancer. And it had claimed her quickly, which was both cruel and a Godsend at the same time, and all Georgia had been left with was a broken heart and a box full of Amy's memories.

While Amy had suffered, she hadn't had to suffer long, but Georgia had felt like she'd suffered every day since.

'Small mercies,' Amy's mother had said the day before Amy passed. She was referring to the cancer taking Amy so quickly and not letting her suffer for too long. Georgia was so angry with her for not being there until the very end and having no idea what Amy had gone through, that she'd had to walk out of the room, leaving Amy's family to fawn all over her while she had no idea they were even there. And then to make matters worse, they'd fought Georgia through the courts for a piece of Amy's estate.

Georgia shook those bad memories from her head as she dug through the box and discovered the ticket stubs and a signed CD case from when they saw Norah Jones in the concert hall at QPAC. It was their first concert together, their third date, and Georgia had pulled out all the stops to impress Amy back then, calling in some favours to get a backstage meeting with Norah after the concert. Georgia smiled at the memory of the joy on Amy's face as Norah Jones signed her CD. Amy chattered on about that meeting for weeks after and they'd had to buy the same CD twice since thanks to Amy wearing it out and scratching it from overuse.

Thinking about Amy and her Norah Jones CD made Georgia think about Zoe and the connection she had to her dad's cassettes and how sweet that was. Why did all her thoughts turn to Zoe lately?

She tossed the ticket stubs and CD case back into the box and after looking through the small stuff, Georgia pulled out a real estate brochure that was jammed in at the bottom. She unfolded it and flipped through it, stopping at a page where the listing had been circled in black pen.

It was Carramar cottage, perched on the top of that hill, views of green rolling hills for miles. The place Georgia had let herself feel so free with Zoe. The place where none of what Amy had gone through had mattered anymore.

'One day, a B&B' Amy had scrawled in underlined capital letters at the top.

Georgia felt a twinge of sadness in the pit of her stomach. Tears pricked at her eyes and she looked at the framed photo of Amy on the bedside table.

'Is this your doing?' she asked.

As she looked around the room, she realised that it had never been the cottage that had reminded Georgia of Amy. It was the apartment. And she wasn't so sure that was a good thing anymore. She closed the lid of Amy's memory box and stood up. No matter what she was feeling, Elizabeth Creek was no longer an option. Zoe had made her feelings perfectly clear the last time they'd seen each other and Georgia wasn't sure whether time apart might change things.

Her phone buzzed in her pocket and when she pulled it out, she smiled. 'Hey Ren, what's up?'

Just as Ren began to speak, there was a knock on Georgia's door.

'Sorry, Ren. Someone's here. Can I call you back?'

She hung up the phone and hurried to the door. When she opened it, she had to step back in shock. 'Zoe.'

Chapter 52

Zoe had been over and over the things she wanted to say to Georgia for the entire drive to the city. Molly had made her realise that the hurt she thought she was over from her past relationships had never been resolved and that when she'd thought Georgia was going to walk out too, she'd ended it before they'd even had a chance to get going.

The realisation, too, that she could walk away from the family business and let Jack do his own thing had lifted a huge weight off Zoe's shoulders. A few beers and an honest conversation had seen them both finally admit they wanted different things. The big question was whether Zoe had the guts to go out on her own and pursue her dream of using her half-finished social work degree and teaching troubled teens to make things out of timber. There was only one way to find out and that was to just suck it up and get stuck in.

Two weeks after she'd started the ball rolling on her new business, Zoe had realised something was missing. Or rather, someone. When she'd stood in the old shed at the cottage, arms crossed, visualising her new workshop, she'd realised it just wouldn't be the same without Georgia. So, she'd thrown an overnight bag into the back of her Landcruiser and made the trip to the city, hoping to win Georgia back.

And now that she stood in Georgia's doorway, seeing the shocked look on Georgia's face, the only thing she could think of to do was to kiss her. So she did.

When she pulled away, she said, 'Sorry, I—' but Georgia didn't let her get anything else out. She grabbed Zoe by the shirt and pulled her into the apartment and kissed her back, hard.

When Georgia finally pulled away, Zoe leaned her head on Georgia's forehead. 'I'm so sorry.'

'Me too,' Georgia replied.

'I said some shitty things,' Zoe said.

'Me too,' Georgia replied. 'You were right about me not letting Amy go.'

Zoe shook her head. 'I shouldn't have said that.'

Georgia smiled. 'Probably not, but I think I needed to hear it.'

'Well, you were right about me and Jack and the whole family business thing,' Zoe said.

'Really?'

'We've made some big changes, actually.'

'I heard,' Georgia replied, walking away into the kitchen. 'Do you want a drink?'

'I'd love one,' Zoe replied, taking the beer Georgia handed her.

'So,' Georgia said, as she walked over to the lounge and sat down. 'You're working for Rick now. That must be a bit of a change.'

Zoe sat down beside her, relaxing back into the cushions. 'Actually, Jack's working for Rick. I'm going out on my own.'

'Oh? You found somewhere to hold your classes?' Georgia asked.

'I did,' Zoe replied. 'I bought the cottage.'

Georgia looked surprised. 'You bought it?'

'I did,' Zoe replied.

'Good for you,' Georgia said and she sounded genuinely happy for Zoe.

'Thanks,' Zoe replied. She twisted her drink in her hand. 'That's sort of why I'm here, actually.'

Zoe swallowed down the nerves that had started kicking around in her stomach and took a long drink from her bottle, some liquid courage, hoping she could remember what she wanted to say. 'You know I'm not that good at business stuff, that's Jack's domain, and well, you know I'm much better with my hands.'

The corner of Georgia's mouth turned up and she arched an eyebrow.

Zoe rolled her eyes, slightly embarrassed. 'You know what I mean.'

'I do,' Georgia replied, the grin not leaving her face.

'Well, anyway, now I have my own business, I have no idea what I'm doing really and I was hoping that maybe you might want to, you know, help me out?'

Georgia sucked in a breath and let it out. 'You want me to be your business partner?'

Zoe shook her head. This wasn't going the way she thought it would. 'No, that's not what I mean.' She rubbed the back of her head, trying to find the right words. Finally, she realised that she just needed to come out and say it. She took in a deep breath and let it out, and looked Georgia in the eyes. 'Living in the cottage won't be the same without you. I was hoping you'd come and live with me. In the cottage.'

Georgia shifted in the chair.

'I mean, it doesn't have to be straight away, obviously, and you can think about it if you need to,' Zoe said, the words tumbling out. 'But that cottage is as much yours as mine, and I know, I *know* it was meant to be for you and Amy, and that you probably need more time to get over that, and I'm prepared to wait, I really am, but—'

'Zoe,' Georgia said, placing her hand on Zoe's knee.

'Yeah?'

'Do you want me to answer or not?'

Zoe nodded, swallowing hard.

A slow smile spread across Georgia's face. 'Are you sure?'

'Do you think I would've driven all the way here and braved the lunatic city drivers if I wasn't sure?' Zoe asked.

Georgia smiled. 'Jack isn't going to want to burn me at the stake? I know what small towns are like.'

Zoe laughed. 'We're not that sort of town. Besides, it's Molly you have to worry about. Maybe don't eat anything she cooks for a while.'

Georgia grinned. 'I'll make sure I don't.'

'So does that mean you're saying yes?' Zoe asked. She held her breath, waiting for Georgia's answer.

Georgia nodded and before she could get out the words, Zoe kissed her, and Georgia kissed her back. When they pulled apart, Georgia said, 'Do you have a business plan I can look at?'

'A business plan?' Zoe asked.

'If I'm going to be helping you run your business, I need to see a business plan,' Georgia said.

Zoe poked Georgia's chest lightly with her finger. 'That's what your job is now.'

'Oh? And what's yours?' Georgia asked, grabbing Zoe's finger and pulling her hand down to touch her thigh.

Zoe grinned mischievously and gently pushed Georgia down on the lounge. 'Making you happy.'

Georgia lifted her head so their lips were barely touching. 'I can run with that.'

Chapter 53

Three months at the cottage and Georgia still had trouble waking up as early as Zoe. She'd never been an early riser if she could help it, but watching the sun rise on the deck with Zoe had become a morning ritual, so she was trying to make waking up early a new habit.

The bunkhouse renovations were in full swing, and Zoe had almost finished setting up her new workshop in the other shed. She was due to hold her first class at the end of the month, which she was excited about and had convinced Dallas to help out on weekends. Zoe would need the extra pair of hands since Nick and Tara had gone travelling overseas. Even the carpet python that Georgia had made homeless was back, finding a new home in the rafters of Zoe's workshop.

With Jack and Rick working so closely together in Rick's business now, Molly and Ren had become friends, with Ren even trying to convince Molly to move them all to Brisbane. They were all due out to Carramar over the coming weekend for the official house warming, and while Georgia was looking forward to seeing them all, she much preferred the quiet time she had at the cottage with Zoe.

She leaned back into the chair and sipped her coffee. It was hard to believe sometimes that she got to live in such a beautiful place. Amy certainly knew what she was doing when she bought this place.

'Hey,' Zoe said, kissing the top of Georgia's head.

'Hey yourself,' Georgia replied as she turned her attention to the table. 'An omelette today?'

'Thought I'd make something special,' Zoe said. 'I have a surprise for you.' She handed Georgia a gift wrapped box. 'Remember when we found the old name plate for the cottage?'

Georgia nodded.

'Well, I know we didn't end up discussing a new name for the place, and I hope you don't mind, but I sort of came up with one myself,' Zoe said.

'What did you call it?' Georgia asked.

'You'll see,' Zoe winked.

She looked quite proud of herself, Georgia thought as she pulled the wrapping off and when she opened the box, she gasped. Tears welled up in her eyes as she pulled the routed timber sign from the box and lay it on her lap. 'Did you make this?' she asked, her voice a whisper.

'Do you like it?' Zoe asked.

'I love it,' Georgia replied. 'But are you sure this is what you want to call our cottage?'

Zoe nodded. 'Definitely. Amy's as much a part of this place as we are.'

Georgia drew in a shaky breath and let it out, as she ran her fingers over the letters on the sign. 'Amy's Rest is perfect.'

The End

A Note from the Author

I hope you enjoyed reading Amy's Rest as much as I enjoyed writing it. It always amazes me where ideas can spring from, and this one came from a conversation I have with my wife every now and again about how we would cope if the other were to die. As morbid as it might sound, it's actually quite comforting to know that your partner just wants you to be happy, and that's what I wanted to write about in Amy's Rest.

Georgia and Zoe are both dealing with grief but in vastly different ways and it was interesting to me, during the course of writing their story, how they dealt with that grief and each other. And of course I couldn't resist throwing in some good old Aussie humour.

When I started out, Amy's Rest was meant to be a single, stand-alone book, but once I began writing about Elizabeth Creek, I realised there were more stories to be told. I can't say too much at the moment, but I have at least three more stories set in Elizabeth Creek that are percolating away. If you want to know when they're ready, be sure to jump on to my mailing list, so you'll be the first to know.

And if you have a few minutes, I'd love an honest review on the site you bought Amy's Rest from.

Reviews help readers find books they love and encourage new readers to take a chance on authors they might not have tried before. Even a short note on what you thought about the books you read makes a huge difference, and of course, each and every review I get means a lot to me, so thank you so much if you write one!

If you want to get in touch with me directly, you can do that via email or social media. I love hearing from readers and answer every message and email I get. I am most active on Twitter and Facebook, and can be found posting pictures of my dogs, coffee and homebrew on Instagram.

Thanks for reading!

Acknowledgements

There are always a lot of people involved in writing my books, from answering small questions to digging me out of major plot holes to pushing me forward and giving me the motivation to keep going.

Huge thanks to Alison Bedford as always, for keeping me on track with this, my first foray into adult fiction. Your ideas and subtle nudges and not-so-subtle suggestions have made the book much better than it would have been without you.

Thank you to Diana King for helping me name Elizabeth Creek. Anyone who has ever heard me talking about my writing knows naming people and things is not my strong point, so I'm extremely grateful to you for saving me from pulling my hair out finding just the right name for the small Australian town that became Elizabeth Creek.

Michael Wait deserves special mention. Although the specifics of cars aren't mentioned too much in any of my books, you're always my go-to car guy when I need to know what sort of car my characters would drive. It makes it even better that I can give you a vague description of a character and you nail their vehicular choice every time.

To my first readers and Aussie author mates, Sophie, KJ, Camryn and Lesley whose comments and encouragement guided me through the uncharted waters of adult lesfic and made the journey so much easier, I owe you all a beer next time we see each other. My betas are getting way too numerous to name individually now, but you know who you are, and I can't ever say it enough - your enthusiasm for my new books every time you read one keeps me going.

To every reader who has taken my stories and characters to heart and loved them as much as I do, if not more, thank you too - you are the reason I write.

And finally, as always, to my wife, Teresa, whose unwavering faith and support (along with the constant dirty looks when I'm not at my laptop) propels me forward into each new bookish adventure.

About the Author

S.R. Silcox started writing sweet romance stories for lesbian teens because she never got to read them when she was younger.

She quickly discovered it was a great way for her to relive her glory days from her childhood and make up for all the things she didn't do but wished she could have.

Like kiss cute girls and play professional cricket.

She currently writes sweet romances for lesbian tweens and teens, as well as the Alice Henderson series about girls who play cricket.

Amy's Rest is her first adult lesbian fiction novel.

She mostly hangs out on Twitter and Instagram, where she posts updates on her new house, sport, her dogs and trying to kick her procrastination habit.

She lives on the coast in (mostly) sunny Queensland, Australia with her wife and two dogs.

https://www.srsilcox.com
https://twitter.com/srsilcox
https://www.instagram.com/srsilcox
http://bit.ly/amysrestnews